The 2:00 a.m. call from her fiancé, Jim, sets Jennifer onto a story that almost ends in disaster. Natalia and Sergei are alone in a strange country they have chosen to call their own. But the young Russian defectors turn up missing and, when found, demand that *Chicago Day* columnist Jennifer Grey be at all their meetings with the authorities. Will they be spirited back to Russia? Will the tension between Jennifer and Jim ever resolve?

Jerry B. Jenkins, is the author of more than ninety books, including the popular Margo Mystery Series, co-author of the best-selling *Out Of The Blue* with Orel Hershiser, and *Hedges*. Jenkins lives with his wife, Dianna, and three sons at Three-Son Acres, Zion, Illinois.

Jerry B. Jenkins

THE CALLING

Book Five In The Jennifer Grey Mystery Series

Flip over for another great
Jennifer Grey Mystery!
VEILED THREAT

BARBOUR BOOKS
Westwood, New Jersey

Copyright © MCMXCI   Barbour and Company, Inc.
P.O. Box 1219
Westwood, New Jersey 07675
All Rights Reserved
Printed in the United States of America
ISBN 1-55748-168-7
91 92 93 94   95   5 4 3 2 1

THE CALLING

One

Her high heels echoed eerily in the frigid parking lot beneath her apartment building. Jennifer Grey could see her breath as she dug for the keys to her Camaro.

Strange, it was even colder in the car. She started the engine and tugged the hood of her down-filled coat up around her head while she let the car idle a bit.

It wasn't like Jim to call her out in the middle of the night, especially a night like this. Late January. Chicago. Two degrees below zero. And chill factor thirty-five below. Temperature on the windshield of a sleek car doing fifty miles an hour down Lake Shore Drive? Nearly incalculable.

Jim had sounded so earnest, so excited, so urgent. "Don't ask any questions, Jenn," he said. "I need you to meet me at Rasto's as soon as you can. Don't tell anyone you're coming."

"The motel?"

"Yes!"

"The one down there, uh—"

"South on the Drive, yes! Hurry, Jennifer."

"Jim, what time is it?"

"I don't know. C'mon! You know I wouldn't ask you if it wasn't important."

"Jim, I can't meet you at a motel in the middle of the night. It would look terrible."

"I'm not alone, sweetheart," he said. "Room fifty-eight, all the way around the back, park in front and walk."

"Who's there with you?"

"Jennifer, please!" And he hung up.

At least he hadn't sounded in trouble. If he had, she wouldn't have taken the time to comb out her long brown hair and apply her makeup. The invitations had gone out two weeks before, and the wedding was less than a month away, but there was no way Jim Purcell was going to see her at less than her best until he had to.

As she pulled out onto the street and headed toward Lake Shore Drive, Jennifer glanced at her watch. Two-thirty. Jim was still on duty, she

4 Jennifer Grey Mysteries

remembered. This would be unique. Not since she had been a *Chicago Day* rookie police reporter and he a Chicago Police Department precinct deskman had she seen him while he was on duty.

Now she was a front-page columnist, and he was about to be named a detective sergeant. *Whatever he wants, it must be important*, she decided. Anyway, she wanted to see him, anytime, all the time, anywhere.

Thinking of Jim almost made her quit wondering what he was up to. Tall, whitish blond hair, pale blue eyes, trim, soft-spoken, serious, devout, considerate. She had to admit he reminded her—except in looks—of her first husband. But she rarely mentioned that to Jim.

She would be glad when Jim was a plainclothes detective, and not just because he would be through with those crazy eleven to seven hours. It was simply that despite all the years and the living alone and the counsel of her father, Jennifer couldn't shake the memories that were stirred by the sight of a young policeman in uniform.

It had been a very young state trooper who had come to her door with the news that her husband of less than a year had been killed in a car accident. She had done well, considering. She was fortunate to have close friends, a good church, a tight family.

But she had never quite gotten over the impact of the police uniforms. She had forced herself to put it out of her mind while on the police beat, but even then, the younger men—the ones who kept their uniforms and shoes and leather belts and holsters spotless—they were the ones who transported her back to the painful memories.

But now she felt privileged. After having decided that she could never fall in love again, it had happened.

She was helplessly, hopelessly, totally in love. It had happened so gradually, so methodically, so certainly, and in such an unlikely way that when she and Jim realized it, they knew it was right.

It wasn't as if they hadn't had problems. Their relationship had been tested from the beginning when Jim was implicated in a scandal and charged in an Internal Affairs Division shakeup.

He was cleared, of course, but the ordeal only drew Jim and Jennifer closer together. Recently, though, another problem had arisen. Just a few weeks before the wedding, Jim decided that God had called him and Jennifer into missionary work.

She wanted to pass it off as immaturity on Jim's part. But that was inconsistent with his character. Maybe *she* was the immature one. Maybe she wasn't spiritual enough to be open to what God might be telling them.

The Calling 5

She would never forget the Thursday night Jim told her. They had been attending their church's missionary conference, a week of famous speakers who were there to get the congregation fired up about missions.

Jennifer had always been interested in missions. Some of her childhood friends were missionaries. She sent them money every month. She also contributed to her denomination's missions program. She had even visited missionaries both times she'd traveled outside the United States.

She had never felt called to serve, but she wasn't closed to that either. At least, maybe not until now. And she didn't know why. When she had been at her most tender point in her relationship with God, she had told Him that she would do whatever He wanted.

At that point, He had brought Scott Grey into her life. Her job then, she felt, was to follow his lead.

Scott was a quiet man, always looking for ways to serve God through his church. He was so old-fashioned that he didn't want Jennifer to work, not that he would have stood in her way if she'd wanted to. In a way she did want to, but she knew she would have to get used to being at home when they started a family, so she didn't look for a job.

She was soon bored and threw herself into more church activities than even Scott could keep up with. They had begun talking seriously about starting a family when he was killed.

Even with the heater on full blast, Jennifer was cold. Maybe it was the wind chill. More likely, it was the memories. She saw the billboard—the only one Rasto's had ever rented—that told her the dingy little motel was still eleven miles south. The only other drivers on the road at that time of the morning were cops, cabbies, drunks, or truckers; but no trucks were allowed on the Drive. Jennifer assumed there weren't too many young women rendezvousing with their young men either.

She could hardly get over how differently she was approaching marriage the second time around. She and Jim had talked very little about starting a family. She didn't know what she would have thought if he had resented her working or just didn't want her to for some reason.

Admittedly, her work had left less time for church work, but she was still as active as possible. She would give up her job for a family too, but now that she was in her thirties, it was something they'd have to discuss.

She had never dreamed of becoming a daily columnist, but it had certainly given her a platform from which to speak out about ethics and social problems from a Christian perspective. In many ways, she felt her job was almost a ministry.

Jim hadn't even suggested she give it up for homemaking. They agreed that if they had a family, she wouldn't work until the youngest was in school.

Jennifer Grey Mysteries

But now, with Jim's seeming call to missionary work, Jennifer's future was less secure and more indefinite than it had been since Scott had died.

She had always assumed that God called people to His service individually.

Sure, if He calls a man, his wife will go along. But what happens when the man is called and the woman isn't his wife yet? And she doesn't sense the same call? In fact, it makes her nervous. Makes her second-guess herself. Makes her question whether she would really follow her love anywhere, at any price. And what a price!

Was she reluctant to consider giving up her job just because it paid more than twice what Jim's paid? Or would she miss seeing her face on the front page of the *Chicago Day* five times a week?

Jennifer should have realized something was different about Jim when they left the church during the missionary conference eight days before. Usually, Jim was eager to get out of the pew and start circulating. He liked to greet people, to ask about them, and—he admitted—to be asked about the upcoming wedding.

Then in the car, he would usually try to engage Jennifer in a discussion of how the meeting, particularly the message, applied to their lives, their jobs, their futures.

But that Thursday night Jim was strangely quiet at the end of the service. When she gathered up her things, she realized he hadn't even stood yet.

She turned to him and smiled, as if to ask if he were ready to leave. Jim looked at her, wide-eyed, as if trying to communicate something—something he apparently thought she should be able to read on his face.

But she couldn't. He almost appeared overcome, but rather than concerning her, it embarrassed her. And that troubled Jennifer. She knew she shouldn't care what other people thought, especially if Jim had something on his mind.

But all she could think of was that people who knew them, the friends who would be coming to their wedding, might think there was something wrong between them.

Jennifer stood and moved toward the aisle, feeling terribly self-conscious when Jim remained seated, staring at her. She glanced back and let her smile fade to a puzzled look and then almost a scowl. It was as if she were willing him to stand and come with her. Finally, he did.

"What's the matter, Jim?" she whispered as he joined her.

"In the car," he said huskily.

It was unlike him to be coy with her. He wasn't a game player, and he had never been brusque. But as they wormed their way out of the crowded

The Calling

7

church, Jim just stared straight ahead, merely nodding to anyone who greeted him.

Jennifer tried to cover for him by becoming more gregarious than normal. But Jim's gentle pressure on her arm urged her out to the car.

"Did I do something to upset you?" she asked as he opened the door for her.

He shook his head, but he didn't speak. Jennifer decided that when the time was right, he would tell her what was wrong. She wasn't going to push him. But by the time he stopped at her apartment, she feared she had made the wrong decision. He had said nothing for almost an hour.

Rather than seeing her to her door, as was his usual custom, Jim led her to the end of the hall where a small couch sat by the windows in a sitting room near the stairwell. He unbuttoned his coat and sat on the edge of the couch, elbows on his knees and hands clasped.

"I really got blitzed tonight," he said finally, so soft she almost couldn't hear.

"He really got to you, huh?" Jennifer said, referring to the speaker.

"It wasn't him so much as the Lord speaking to me," Jim said.

Jennifer was taken aback. Jim was a very spiritual guy, a Sunday school teacher and a deacon. But it was rare that he ever said such things. "About missions?" she asked.

He nodded. "About being a missionary."

She froze. Was he serious? "About your being a missionary?" she asked, wishing he'd simply been inspired to give more money, or whatever.

He shook his head. "Us. Both of us."

She nodded slightly and looked away.

"Better pray about it, Jennifer," he said.

"You took my very words," she said.

"You know what this would mean for our careers."

She didn't even move. When he said no more, she put a hand on his shoulder. "Let's talk about it when you've had more time to think about it."

Jim answered, "I'll never waver from this, Jennifer. It's of God."

Again, his vocabulary jangled in her ears. In a way, she had always wished he felt more comfortable talking about the Lord, but this was weird. She didn't like it. It didn't make sense. It was all coming too fast.

"I'll talk to you tomorrow," she said.

He looked quickly at her, as if surprised that she was unwilling to discuss it right then. "Too tired right now?" he asked. She nodded and stood. He followed her to her door. "I won't be tired for a week," he said.

She feared he was speaking the truth.

For the next several days their conversations were the same. Jim felt God was trying to tell him something. That he was supposed to give up his

8 Jennifer Grey Mysteries

job, his career, his life-style, and go to Bible school. He was to prepare for missionary work.

They had hardly ever argued about anything, and Jennifer certainly didn't want to start with something as crucial as this. She remained guarded, almost aloof. She knew it was frustrating for him, but she couldn't even nod in agreement without his assuming that she was buying the whole package.

He never said it in so many words, but she got the impression that he thought she should share the vision, quit her job, and follow him to wherever God would lead.

When she asked a probing question or two, implying that maybe he should back away a bit and get counsel from trusted friends about such a decision, she sensed it almost angered him. In a way, she hoped he would hit a boiling point. She wanted it all out, but she knew if she angrily confronted him about it, it would appear she was not open to God's leading.

And she was. She thought.

A week and a day after the Thursday night meeting, Jennifer pulled off Lake Shore Drive and into the parking lot of a seedy motel where she was to meet her fiancé. And who knew who else? Or for what reason?

Two

Not even Rasto's was hopping at that time of the morning. Jennifer wheeled to the end of the first two-story wing of rooms and parked in the shadows.

The long drive had made the car toasty, and she had been able to take off her gloves, lower her hood, and unbutton her coat. But as soon as she stepped out into the air, she turned her back to the icy wind and hunched her shoulders, ducking to bring the hood back up while she quickly buttoned her coat and fumbled for her gloves.

As she walked across the parking lot and past two more buildings, she wished she had worn quieter heels and had brought a smaller handbag. She stopped and looked behind her every twenty or so steps, and her handbag slid off her shoulder or banged her hip each time.

She heard nothing but the wind with her hood up. But that crazy, irrational fear that comes with hurrying through a dimly lit parking lot in the middle of the night and in the dead of winter made her heart crash against her ribs.

Jennifer had been to Rasto's only once, and then only for a clandestine meeting in the parking lot for a story she had written while on the police beat. The contact person turned out to be a phony, and the story never ran in the paper, but Jennifer never forgot the almost unbelievable tackiness of the place.

Many times she had pointed out the motel to Jim as they flew by on the Drive. It almost became an inside joke with them. If she neglected to notice it, he'd remind her, "That was the place that you met the guy who didn't pan out and—"

"Yeah, yeah," she'd say, mimicking how he reacted when she pointed it out to him.

Jennifer determined where room 58 would be by a process of elimination. Only every second or third sign telling which rooms were where had survived the vandals and the years, so when she reached the back of the last row of rooms, she edged away from the crumbly walkway and out into the parking lot to squint up at the second floor.

9

10 Jennifer Grey Mysteries

There were no lights in the parking lot back there, and only a few lights were working outside the rooms. She saw room 51 at one end and 60 at the other, but no other numbers were visible. The only room with a light shining from the inside of closed drapes was the third from the right end, the one she assumed had to be 58.

She edged back closer to the building and felt her way to the outside stairwell. The wrought iron steps seemed to almost give way as she gingerly, and not too quietly, trotted up to the cement platform leading to the rooms.

She would rather have taken the steps more slowly and carefully to ensure against tripping, but she decided the risk was worth it to get on a flat surface again. The stairwell was pitch dark, and she imagined hands darting toward her legs as she moved up the steps.

She slowed and tried to catch her breath as she walked toward the room with the light. Just as she leaned close to see if she could make out the number, the light went out, and she heard the door jerk open just far enough to pull against the chain.

She gasped.

"Jenn?" Jim whispered.

"Yes," she mouthed, but no sound came.

"Yes," she tried again, squeaking it out.

The light came on, the chain came off, and Jim, in his stocking feet and street clothes, reached out to pull her in. "Anybody out there?" he asked, still whispering.

"I hope not," she said, moving toward him and expecting a warming embrace. He edged past her and flipped the light off again, sticking his head out the door to watch and listen. She hadn't noticed anyone in the room, but a second after Jim darkened the room, she noticed a light go off under the door to the bathroom.

Jim pulled back in and shut the door, and in the darkness she heard him set the lock in the knob and reattach the chain before he turned the light back on. As he fussed with the drape to be sure it fully covered the window, she finally got a good look at him. His hair was mussed, his collar unbuttoned, his tie loose.

He placed both a cheap, rickety chair and a heavy table up against the door, a thick green ashtray sliding around as he moved the table. Then he looked Jennifer full in the face with that same smile of wonder and excitement she had noticed in the church a week before and came to her. She withdrew her clenched, gloved hands from deep in her pockets and held him.

The Calling

The room was cold, and the heater was laboring. "Ooh, you're freezing," he said, pressed against her coat. But he didn't pull away for a few seconds. "Sit down," he said finally.

She looked around and noticed that the room's only chair was the one Jim had pressed into service as a door stop. She sat on the edge of one of the two double beds set a couple of feet away from each other.

She lowered her hood and shook out her hair, and her hands found their way back into her pockets and she sat with her knees and ankles pressed together for warmth. Jim deftly crawled atop the other bed and sat Indian style facing her.

"Still cold?" he asked.

She nodded, smiling only slightly. She wasn't going to beg, but her reporter's curiosity was about to get the better of her. She wished he'd get on with it.

Jim took a deep breath and looked at the ceiling, then back at her. "There's someone I'd like you to meet."

"I gathered that," she said.

"But first I have to tell you about them."

"Them?"

"Them. There are two. A boy and a girl."

"Kids or a couple?"

"Both."

"Both? You mean four?"

"No, two kids. A couple. They're about twenty-one, I guess."

She wanted to ask who they were, where they were, where he'd met them, and why they were holed up here. Not to mention why he wasn't in uniform on a work night. But she got the impression he wanted her to ask all that, one question at a time, and she wasn't in the mood for the game.

"You won't believe it," he said, pausing. She assumed he was trying to get her to keep pumping him. He couldn't. "They're from Russia. The Soviet Union."

"What are they doing here?" she asked, unable to stifle the question.

"They escaped! They're seeking political asylum."

"What are you doing with them?"

"Hiding them. We have reason to believe the KGB is after them, and the last thing they want to do is be dragged back."

"Start from the beginning, Jim. I don't get this."

"Fred and I were on patrol when we got a call to ten-nineteen the station and ten-twenty-five the captain."

"It's been too long, Jim. Refresh me."

"Return to the station and meet with the captain."

"For what?"

12   Jennifer Grey Mysteries

"That's what we wanted to know. I mean, we've got a watch commander, the sergeant. His boss, a lieutenant, certainly doesn't work the graveyard shift. And they want us to come in and see a captain at midnight?"

Jennifer took her gloves off and entwined her fingers, leaning forward toward Jim.

"So we get there, and there's Captain Bram with the lieutenant and our watch commander. We figure maybe we're in trouble for something, you know?"

"*Norman* Bram?"

"The one and only."

"How long's he been a captain? Seems only yesterday he was still a sergeant."

"Well, he was made lieutenant just after you became a columnist, and he was made captain during the new commissioner's shakeup."

"Must be nice. He couldn't have been a lieutenant for even a year."

"Nine months to the day. Anyway, he's all serious and everything—they all are—and he invites us into this training room."

"Not his office?"

"Nope. That big schoolroom-like place where they train cadets."

Jennifer nodded.

"Bram motions for us to pull chairs up around the table at the front of the room, and he sits on the table. By now we're really scared, and I can tell Fred's thinkin' the same thing I am, that we messed up somehow, and royally. I couldn't think of anything we'd done wrong, but I was sure my promotion was down the tubes.

"Bram tells us they've gotten a call from federal agents in Detroit. Seems this young Russian couple—they're not married, but they will be soon—had escaped the Soviet Union through Canada somehow and made it all the way to Detroit. They turned themselves in and were protected by federal agents for a couple of days before it was determined that no one was following them. Then they were freed."

The room was warming, and so was Jennifer. She shed her coat and kicked off her shoes.

"They took a bus to Chicago late last night, and a couple of hours after they'd left Detroit, the feds were tipped that three Soviet diplomats—ones they had been carefully watching for a year—had been seen in the bus station that night."

"The agents think these guys are spies?"

The Calling

"They thought they might be. But now they suspect they're KGB. Well, they didn't have time to fly to Chicago to protect the kids, so they got hold of the federal office in Chicago, who asked us to protect them for a while."

"While *they* do what?"

"The feds?"

"Uh-huh."

"Handle the KGB, I guess. So Fred and I were told to change into our street clothes and take our own car—we took Fred's—and meet these two as they got off the bus in Chicago. That was easy enough, but they were scared to death when we approached them. We had trouble convincing them we were really American policemen and not KGB until we told them the names of the agents who had protected them in Detroit."

"So, why didn't you take them to the police station?"

"They'd be too easy to find. We were supposed to find a remote, unpopular, and not auspicious place to hole up for a while."

"You sure found it."

"It was the first place I thought of, Jennifer. You know, this is the place you—"

"Yeah, yeah. Where's Fred?"

"Home. He's gonna relieve me in the morning. But there's no way I'm going to sleep, and I knew you'd want to meet them."

"I do, but I suppose everything has to be off-the-record and that if I write anything at all about them, you're in big trouble."

"Nope. Just the opposite."

Jennifer stood. "You're kidding."

"I'm not."

She paced. "We've both been warned, you by your bosses and me by mine. You can't give me scoops."

"This is an exception."

"Why?"

"'Cause Bram says so. Why do you think they just happened to choose Fred and me for this assignment, of all the guys on the street tonight?"

"They chose you for me?"

"You got it."

"Bram has that authority?"

"Right from the top."

"The commissioner?"

Jim nodded, still in a cross-legged position, smiling up at Jennifer. "Apparently, the feds say the best thing we can do for these kids—now that the USSR is on to them—is to make them visible, not to the KGB, but to the public."

14   Jennifer Grey Mysteries

"In other words, get some good quotes from them so there would be a real outcry if the KGB tried to say they were coerced or kidnapped or brainwashed?"

"I guess."

"Too good to be true."

"Jennifer, I hope you care as much about them as about the columns they might be worth."

"You know I do."

"No, I don't."

She smiled. "I don't either. But I can be won over. Get them out here. They must be boiling in that bathroom."

"You kiddin'? That's the coldest room in the place."

"Sergei!" Jim called. "Natalya! Come on out!"

Indeed, a cold blast of air greeted Jennifer when the young couple emerged. They both wore short, dark ski-type jackets, jeans, and leather boots. Sergei Baranov was a tall, rangy, bony boy with fair skin and dark hair. His cold, black eyes belied the expectant expression on his face. He seemed genuinely pleased to shake hands with Jennifer.

Natalya Danilin hung back, almost hiding behind her boyfriend. But Jennifer gently tugged the tiny girl toward her when Natalya offered her hand, and they embraced awkwardly.

The girl's eyes were a translucent hazel, and while her hair was almost a nondescript brown, her long nose, pearly teeth, and full lips made her stunningly pretty, especially when she smiled.

"We would love to talk to you at length," Sergei said, his voice low, his accent thick, but his English perfect. "It means security for us. But we are so tired. We have not slept well. I don't believe we are up to it yet."

Jennifer was glad she hadn't reached for her notebook when Jim first told her she could interview them. "I understand," she assured them. Natalya looked relieved. She sighed.

"As long as I can talk to you before four o'clock tomorrow afternoon," Jennifer said. "We can get something in the weekend papers. And the Sunday editions have the most readers."

"Big paper?" Sergei asked.

"Biggest in Chicago."

"Bigger than the *Tribune*?" he asked, surprising her.

"As of last fall, yes," she said. "*The Chicago Day*."

"New," he said. "News of it has not reached our country."

"It will soon enough," Jennifer said.

Three

Patrolman Fred Bishop, a thick, balding, forty-five-year-old double divorcé who aspired to little beyond his current job, tapped on the window at ten-thirty that morning. Jim leaped to his feet, his snub-nosed revolver seeming to jump from an ankle holster into his hand.

He peeked through the curtain and unlocked the door. Bishop backed through the door, laden with steaming styrofoam boxes. "Hungry, comrades?" he asked. Jim winced at his crudeness, shushed him, and pointed to the beds. Sergei and Natalya, still in their clothes, lay sleeping in each. Jennifer had been napping on the floor between the beds.

"The smell of the food will wake them soon enough," Jennifer said, greeting Bishop, who pretended to be surprised to see her, yet had known to bring her breakfast. He usually liked to flirt with her, in front of Jim or not, and she was just as accustomed to ignoring him. She hoped Jim would stay around until she was finished interviewing the Russians, but she knew he needed to get home for some rest before standing guard again that night.

The squeaking of the boxes made Natalya sit up, and for a moment she look scared and puzzled. "How 'bout a scrambled egg, Olga?" Bishop asked, displaying a forkful.

She squinted at him and mouthed, "Olga?"

Jennifer scowled at Fred and motioned for Natalya to join them. The tiny girl scooted to the end of the bed, stretched, and let her legs dangle. Jennifer handed her a fast-food breakfast and a small cup of coffee.

Natalya said something in Russian, then realized that no one awake could understand. "Hungry," she said, smiling at Jennifer. Fred laughed loud, and her smile faded. Already it was apparent she didn't know what to make of him.

Sergei rolled onto his back, and Jim stood with another box. But Natalya, her mouth full, waved at Jim and shook her head. "Not awake," she said. Sergei snored.

"He'll be hungry," Jim whispered. "And this won't stay hot long."

"Hot, cold," she said. "Never mind to Sergei. He not sleep well for many nights. He must feel safe here."

15

16 Jennifer Grey Mysteries

"He'd better!" Bishop said. "He's got Chicago's finest lookin' out for the Russian goons!"

Jennifer put a finger to her lips, and Natalya wondered aloud, "Goons?"

"He means the KGB," Jim said. "It's just an expression."

"Goons," she repeated softly. Gobbling her food, she was quickly finished and drank the rest of her steaming coffee in a few gulps. "I take shower?" she asked, rummaging through her backpack for a change of clothes.

Jim nodded, and she headed toward the bathroom.

"You need any help, you let Fred know, hear?" Bishop said, grinning and winking at her. Natalya looked puzzled again, and Jim and Jennifer quickly chastised him.

"What's the matter with you?" Jennifer asked.

"Yeah," Jim added. "This is hardly the time or place or person for that."

"Hey, I was only kiddin', all right?"

"Your humor doesn't translate well," Jennifer said. "How's she supposed to know what you meant?"

"She knew well enough; I think she likes me."

Jennifer rolled her eyes and shook her head. When Jim announced that he was leaving to get some sleep and that he would be back for a seven to three shift, she tried to tell him with her eyes that she wished he would stay. But he simply stood, bent to kiss her, and pulled on his coat as he left.

"Should we bolt the door?" Jennifer asked, but knowing as soon as she said it that she had opened herself to one of Bishop's lines.

"Not unless you're afraid of me," he said, grinning.

"If there's anybody I'm not afraid of, Fred, it's you."

He shook his head and turned back to his food. He started to open the one remaining box.

"If that Russky's gonna sleep through chow, I'm havin' his."

"No, you're not, Fred," Jennifer said. "The boy's going to be starving when he wakes up. Just leave it for him." She stared at him until he put the box back down, but like a child who didn't get his own way, he left it open to get cold. Jennifer stood and bolted the door, then closed the breakfast box and put it next to her handbag.

A few minutes later Natalya emerged from the steaming shower, dressed as she had been before but with clean clothes. Her head was wrapped in a towel, and she was vigorously trying to dry her long hair. "Cold in there!" she announced, shutting the door behind her.

"I should have brought my hair dryer," Jennifer said. "You can never go out in this weather if your hair is even damp."

The Calling

17

Natalya looked genuinely shocked. 'What surprises you?" Jennifer asked.

"You think this weather is bad?"

"You said the bathroom was cold," Jennifer said. "You must know it's terrible outside."

"This would be mild in Leningrad. You really have hair dryer?"

"Sure. I'll bring it for you next time I come."

"Then I can go out in your terrible weather with my dry hair?"

Jennifer smiled, but Fred Bishop broke in. "You're goin' nowhere, Olga. Least not till we get clearance from the feds."

"Natalya," Natalya said timidly, pointing to herself.

"Whatever," he said.

"Not everyone in America can pronounce three-syllable words," Jennifer told her. "And if you didn't know any better, you might think that because a famous gymnast was named Olga, all Russian girls are."

"Olga Korbut!" Natalya whispered loudly. "You know Olga!"

"Do you?" Jennifer asked.

"Everybody in homeland knows Olga. Not in person, of course, but yes. You know her?" she added, looking at Fred, who still appeared to be smarting from Jennifer's shot.

"Just from TV," he said. "She was big stuff in Munich in seventy-two, right?"

"Olympics," Natalya said. "I remember well because I was nine then. She became big hero."

"You were nine then?" Bishop said, swearing. "I was still married to my second wife then, but it doesn't seem that long ago."

"Long time," Natalya said. "Olga old married lady now. Almost thirty."

"You're kidding!"

"I'm what?"

"You're joking," he said. "It's an expression."

"Expression," Natalya said. "Like goons?"

"Whatever. Olga's really that old, huh?"

She nodded. "I teach you say *Natalya*, OK?"

"Nah."

"That's good start! Na, tall—"

"Nah! No!"

"Come on! Tal—"

"Natalia, OK?" he blurted.

"No, not four, um—"

"Syllables," Jennifer helped.

"Right. Just three. Na, tal, ya. You try."

18 Jennifer Grey Mysteries

"I don't wanna say yer dumb name. I'll call ya Natalie or Olga, whichever you want. Just quit teaching me."

"Natalie? OK. But not Olga."

"Awright! Hey, when's yer ol' man gonna get up?"

"Old man?"

"Well, he's not yer husband. What is he? Yer lover?"

"Sergei? He'll get up when he's rested."

"Then I'm gonna eat his breakfast."

"Then what will he eat?" Jennifer and Natalya both looked at Bishop, wondering if he had an answer. He didn't. He just waved disgustedly and turned his back on her, then went to peek out the window. The bright morning sun shone directly into Sergei's eyes, and he stirred.

Slowly he sat up. "Officer Bishop," he said thickly. "Good morning to you."

"Good morning to you too, Stosh." Before Sergei could react, Jennifer was yelling at Bishop. "Honestly, Fred, can't you call a person by his name once in your life? You've even got your bigotry mixed up! Stosh is a derogatory nickname for a *Pole*, not a Russian. Is Sergei too hard for you? Two simple syllables—*Sir* and *Gee*. Try it."

"Get off my back, Jennifer, huh?"

"Actually, it's more like *Sare Chee*," Sergei corrected her, a twinkle in his eye. It was obvious he was aware of the tension between Jennifer and Fred, and he enjoyed it. Jennifer liked him already. He wolfed down his breakfast and headed for the shower.

"What are you going to be doing while I'm interviewing these two?" Jennifer asked Fred.

He continued staring out the window. "Watchin' TV, I guess," he said. "*Wide World o' Sports* is on, I think."

"That's going to make it difficult for me to concentrate, Fred. Do you have to?"

"What else am I gonna do, listen in? That would bother you too, wouldn't it?"

"Well, yes."

"Then what am I supposed to do, take a walk? I get myself kidnapped, you wind up dead, and Stosh and Natalie'll be doin' hard labor in Siberia by next week!"

"I thought maybe you'd ignore us and read or something."

"Hey, this is *my* gig, not yours. This interview is a favor to you. What I'm doin' is my job whether I like it or not. It's like guarding the enemy."

"Fred! These kids *left* Russia and are seeking asylum here."

"They could be spies."

The Calling

"Silliness. Spies don't make noise by defecting."

"Hey, Jennifer, why are you on my case today? I always thought we had fun together. What's eatin' you?"

"I've just found you crude and a little prejudiced today, that's all," she said.

"Your man, he's never curt with me. He's always the perfect gentleman."

Jennifer flushed. "Well, I know. And I'm sorry. I should be as nice to you as Jim is. But you're not always the perfect gentleman with me, are you?"

"I try to be. But, hey, you're a good lookin', uh, lady, and any guy likes to have fun with the ladies, right?"

"Well, I'm flattered that you find me attractive, but there are more appropriate ways of expressing it."

"Yeah, well, if I knew more about what was appropriate, I'd still be married, wouldn't I?"

"Perhaps. But I'm sorry, Fred, if I've been nasty to you. I just don't want you giving these kids a hard time, even out of ignorance, OK?"

"So now I'm ignorant."

"That's not what I meant."

"It's what you said."

"I'm sorry."

"That's all right. And speakin' of married, you're next, huh?"

Natalya, who had been pretending not to listen for several minutes, looked at Jennifer.

"Yes, it won't be long," Jennifer told Fred.

"Us too," Natalya said. "Sergei and I want to marry as soon as possible."

"Don't rush into anything," Fred said.

"We are not rushing. We have been promised to each other five years."

"Wow," Fred said. "Maybe you oughta rush into it, huh? Bet you're not a virgin like Jennifer here though, right?"

Jennifer's jaw dropped, and Natalya turned away from Fred, picking up a local restaurant directory and pretending to thumb through it. "You see what I mean, Fred?" Jennifer said. "How can you talk that way to her?"

"Hey, what's wrong with the truth? Isn't that true about you?"

"Fred, my father wouldn't even ask that."

"Why, 'cause he knows better or he's just a classier guy than me?"

"Both."

"See, you're bein' mean to me again. Here I am, all fascinated by this beautiful woman who's still, how to say it, *pure*. And you want to climb on my case."

20   Jennifer Grey Mysteries

"For your information, I happen to be a widow. I saved myself for marriage and was faithful to my husband, as I plan to be with Jim."

"Yeah, but in the meantime you've stayed straight—that's what I can't understand."

"That's true, but it's also none of your business. How do you know what I've been or haven't been?"

"Because Jim talks about you all the time."

"He certainly doesn't talk about *that!*"

"Just once, when I was asking him about himself and how a guy his age could still be, you know, inexperienced. He said that it went along with what you two believe. Sounds pretty boring."

Jennifer hated herself for saying it even before it came out: "But then, divorce is boring too, isn't it?"

"Ouch."

"I shouldn't have said that, Fred. I'm sorry. That was cold."

"But a nice shot. I deserved it. I just always figured maybe you were a fun-loving type, and who knew what kind of a chance I might have, you know?"

Jennifer shrugged, not wanting to appear to condone his behavior now or previously.

Natalya turned to face him. "And that is why you asked me that question?" she asked, eyes flashing. He winked at her. Jennifer shook her head disgustedly. And Natalya said, "Sergei would kill you."

"With what?" Fred asked, turning away from her. Under his breath he muttered, "A hammer and sickle?"

"You're hopeless," Jennifer whispered, and Sergei appeared, drying his short hair.

"You two up to answering a few questions?" Jennifer asked him.

Sergei smiled and in his charming bass voice asked, "Is that your way of asking if we are ready for two hours of questioning?"

Jennifer nodded. Fred Bishop looked annoyed. Sergei and Natalya sat next to each other on one bed, and Jennifer sat facing them on the other. As she pulled her notepad and pen from her handbag, Bishop dragged his chair over in front of the television, turned it away from the others, found his sports show, and put his feet up.

Jennifer was grateful that the sound was low enough not to distract them. Her new friends stared briefly at each other and held hands, then looked at Jennifer without smiling. They were eager to get started.

"Does the name *Chulkov* mean anything to you?" she began.

"Does it mean anything to us?" Sergei repeated. "They were our models. Our idols."

The Calling

"And they were from Leningrad," Natalya added. "Tchaikovsky Street."

"You knew them?" Jennifer asked.

"Never met them," Sergei said. "But we knew people who did. We know their whole story. They are why we escaped. How did you know?"

"Just guessing," Jennifer said. "I read about them and wondered, that's all."

"You want their story the way we heard it?" Sergei asked.

"Precisely."

"OK," he said. "And then you'll want ours."

"Right again."

Four

"Perhaps you should tell us what you know already," Sergei suggested.

"All I know is what I read from the wire services," Jennifer said. "I tried to reach the Chulkovs by phone in England, but I never got to them. A piece was published out of London, and as I recall, they were a young married couple."

"Yes," Natalya said. "Oleg and Irina."

"And he was a sailor with the Russian navy," Jennifer said.

"Fourth officer on the Soviet cargo ship *Mekhanik Evgrafo*," Sergei said. "You'll find we know everything about them. Everything."

Jennifer smiled at the young couple. "All I remember is that he stowed her away on his ship, and they escaped to England."

"Oh, it was much more exciting and romantic than that," Natalya said. "They did it for love. The love of each other."

"And is that true with you as well?"

"Yes and no," Sergei said, and Natalya nodded. "We would have done this had we been just friends or brother and sister. We had wanted to leave Russia long before we met. Just like the Chulkovs."

"He actually stowed her away in his own room on board ship, am I right?"

"Yes, yes," Sergei said. "They did not even tell their families good-bye. They were so tired of the special treatment that was reserved for only those who were active in the party and the four and five hours of standing in line for food. The state makes use of you, Miss Grey. Everyone loves the motherland so much and hates the oppression. Everyone wants to flee, and everyone wants to stay. We will miss so much."

"OK, start at the beginning of Oleg and Irina's story."

Sergei began, "Oleg's mother had been to Britain when he was ten. She was there on a course; she was a teacher. They told her not to return to Russia praising Britain, but she couldn't help herself. She didn't get in trouble for it, but she certainly made her son hunger to see the world. That's why he joined the merchant navy. He saw so much of the world that he knew he must escape. When he fell in love with Irina, he knew he had to find a way to take her with him."

"And he did this how?"

"He only had one place to hide her. Under the bed in his small cabin. There was little more than a foot of space under the bed, and it was taken up by two huge drawers for storage. He smuggled a power saw on board and cut the drawers to half their width, leaving room for Irina when they appeared to push all the way back in."

"How she could stand that for so many days and nights is a mystery to me," Natalya said. "I would not have been able to take it for one hour. People visited his cabin, a maid made up his bed every day, and Irina had to stay there when the ship was in a storm. She could only get out for a short time every few hours."

"It is an amazing story," Sergei said. "When they finally got to England, Oleg told the sailor guarding the gangplank that he could go to bed early because Oleg was not sleepy and would cover for him. As soon as the man was gone, Oleg got Irina, and they jumped to the pier and ran through the rain to the authorities."

Sergei and Natalya were beaming, Natalya on the verge of tears. "We heard and told their story so many times, and we read copies of it that were smuggled in from the West," Natalya said with her thick accent. "No one admits, even to each other, that they envy Oleg and Irina, but many do. And many will try to do as they did."

"How will they do it?"

"The way we did it," Sergei said. "With some variations, of course."

"I'm dying to know," Jennifer said, realizing she had never used that in an interview before.

Natalya looked at Sergei, and he laughed. "Our friends will be shocked."

"Why?"

"They think we hate each other," Natalya said.

"They do?"

"We have pretended to hate each other since we first fell in love."

"I don't understand."

"We met in school. Sergei had moved in from Kiev. All the girls were crazy for him from the beginning."

"But my heart went only to Natalya. Probably because she didn't pursue me."

"All the others went after him, and he ran the other way. I waited for my chance. At last it came."

"When we finally had the chance to talk, someone interrupted, and we ended up arguing. I thought all was lost and that she would never speak to me again. But she started passing me notes."

"How old were you at this time?"

"I was fourteen. He had just turned fifteen. One day we went into the city together, just us two. We went to the park and talked and walked and talked some more. No one saw us. The next day we met again, and we knew something was happening between us. We laughed about how we

24   Jennifer Grey Mysteries

argued the first time and how everyone thought we hated each other, and yet we were starting to care for each other."

"I had started to care long before," Sergei said. "But now it was mutual. When we got serious, we finally admitted to each other our dreams of defecting. We told no one at school that we were seeing each other, and we never let anyone see us together alone."

"During our first year in love, we came up with the plan," Natalya said. "We had been playing this game, pretending we did not care, just so our friends would not tease us and ask questions. Then we decided to use it to make people believe we were enemies."

"For what purpose?"

"To aid in our escape. So we could leave together with no one suspecting."

"I don't understand."

Sergei explained, "The reason that Oleg and Irina Chulkov had to devise such a plan was because they were in love and then they were married. The state watched them carefully. Oleg could not be at sea when his wife was visiting the West on business. So she had to go with him in that very dangerous manner."

"We could not do that," Natalya said. "My Sergei is not a sailor, and I am afraid of closed-in places."

"Claustrophobic."

"Yes. And so all the while—and I mean for many years—Sergei and I played an act in front of everyone, including our families. They all thought we despised each other. And the whole time we were madly in love and had promised ourselves to each other forever."

"I guess I still don't understand how that helped you."

"We had been studying English since our first years in school. When we studied advanced English in later years, no one was suspicious of our being in the same class. We each even convinced everyone that if the other turned up in the same Intourist training program, we would quit. When it happened, Sergei's friends told him to ignore me and not worry. 'So you hate her,' they said. 'So what? Just forget it. She can't hurt you.' Meanwhile, my friends were saying the same things. I told them, 'Do you realize that I might have to travel to another country with that monster? I would not be able to stand that!' And they said, 'Just ignore him.'"

"So you were both studying to be guides for tourists from English-speaking countries?"

"Right."

"And you hoped someone you met would help you defect?"

"No. Too risky," Sergei answered. "Our plan was to travel to other countries on get-acquainted tours and establish that we really couldn't

The Calling 25

tolerate each other. It worked quite well. The instructors counseled both of us to be sure that we didn't let our animosity show through to the tourists or to our hosts in Britain and Canada. In Britain, Natalya purposely got herself in trouble by not returning to the group on time. I had been so convincing in expressing my dislike for her that I was assigned to find her and drag her back. We almost escaped then, but another girl stayed with Natalya, and we wouldn't have succeeded. Anyway, we wanted to get to America, and we didn't know how we would get there from England. It was a perfect rehearsal for Canada though."

"So you had a trip planned to Canada."

"Yes, about a year later. We were both tour guides in Russia, and we saw each other in public occasionally when we had training or short tours. Without overdoing it, we clearly established that we would just as soon not be associated with each other. Privately, we were engaged, of course."

"And you trusted no one with your secret? No one at all?"

"No," Sergei said, but Jennifer sensed he was holding back.

"We can tell you," Natalya said finally, "but you must not write it."

"Fair enough."

"We each had one very close friend who knew. But they did not know each other, and as far as we know they never told anyone else. We trusted them, and they were just as afraid as we were of what might happen if the authorities had known about us."

"Will they be escaping too, or trying to?"

Both shook their heads. "They have their reasons," Sergei said. "But they will not be coming."

Natalya added, "Now because people know they are our friends, they will likely be questioned about our disappearance."

"And they're probably saying that they always thought you hated each other," Jennifer supplied.

"Probably. But they will not be believed, and they will be watched for a long time."

"So how did you finally make it out?"

"The Canadian trip," Sergei said, "was to be the end of our playacting. We became so good at being terrible to each other in public that it became difficult to remain in love in private."

"But we manage," Natalya said.

"Before we left for Canada," Sergei said, "we heard a heavy speech of patriotism. We were reminded that we had been chosen for the Intourist training because we had been good students, industrious citizens, lovers of the motherland. We were reminded also of the basic tenets of communism and the evils of capitalism. That was when I knew we could wait no longer. We had planned for a long time to escape in Canada, but we had

26   Jennifer Grey Mysteries

always held out the possibility that something could go wrong and we would abandon our plans. I remember telling Natalya after that meeting that we would go for it all, no turning back, no matter what. We agreed it was worth the risk."

Natalya nodded.

"What so upset you about that last speech?" Jennifer asked. Natalya started to speak, but couldn't articulate it and yielded to Sergei again.

"Basically, we were told why things that might look attractive in the West were not all they appeared to be. And we were told that we were indeed the most free people on the face of the earth. No one could have believed it, but we all sat there obediently."

"How could they pretend that you were free?"

"I don't know. I think it's because they truly believe that the current dictatorship is still temporary."

"Temporary?"

"Yes, that was Lenin's idea in 1917. The dictatorship was to be a temporary government to rule over the landlords and the overthrown capitalists. This was supposed to make the proletariat and the peasant equal and evolve into a classless society. It has never happened. It never will happen. Lenin actually intended for the state as we know it to become unnecessary and wither away."

"Then how would the republic be governed?"

"If it all worked according to plan, there would be no people governing people, just people governing things and systems."

"Why didn't it work?" Jennifer asked, looking toward Natalya.

"Don't ask me—he is the history expert."

Sergei smiled. "After Lenin died, there was what looked like very successful economic planning. The five-year plan made for a healthy economy. And then the border nations seemed hostile, even though they might say the hostility was coming from our side. So the power of the Soviet state, it seemed to the leaders, had to be increased. There is a pretense of representative government, but all is done for the sake of the state as a whole. Everyone can vote except those who have been declared insane. And if you do not wholly support the party—"

"—you are insane," Natalya finished.

"Right," Sergei said. "Even though the constitution of 1977 says that citizens have the right to profess or not to profess any religion, atheism is a party tenet. Religious instruction is against the law, so what is the future of religion in Russia?"

"Do you care about that?" Jennifer asked.

"Do we care? Of course, we care! I am not an atheist. Natalya is not an atheist."

The Calling

"Forgive me, but I thought you would be."

"I understand, but you might be surprised how few true atheists are in the Soviet Union. Some of the party leaders may really believe they are atheists, but most citizens, like Natalya and me, we are agnostics. Thinking people in the Soviet Union do not agree that there is no God just because the party says so. I know many scientists and scholars who refuse to subscribe to atheism."

"Do you know of any Christians in the Soviet Union?"

"Many! Most are Russian Orthodox, but they cause no trouble. The ones we admire are the radicals, the underground Christians, the ones who meet in homes and in the forests, who risk their freedom and their lives, worshiping and teaching their children. How free is a man who cannot teach his children what he believes most deeply? We had to get out. How free were we that we had to flee through deception?"

"Tell me, Sergei," Jennifer said, "what really happened to people who got out of line?"

"People who resisted the government, you mean? Who acted independently, as if they really had the freedoms the constitution promises?"

Jennifer nodded.

"KGB."

"KGB what?"

"KGB is the answer to opposition. The secret police of the committee of state security. They are big, widespread, and have tremendous power."

Natalya pulled her feet up under her and clasped her hands in front of her knees. "Do you know that I had been in love with Sergei for a year before I was entirely sure he was not KGB?"

"You're serious?"

"Absolutely."

"I feared the same of her," Sergei said. He poked her. "And you shouldn't be so sure now, my love."

Natalya laughed a hollow laugh. "Many in Russia do not trust their own families. Anyone can be KGB."

"What can they do to you?"

"The most common punishment for betraying the motherland is hard labor at one of the camps in Siberia that Russian history will tell you were closed in the nineteen fifties."

"And that's what you risked by defecting?"

"Fifteen years hard labor is lenient," Sergei said.

"How severe can it be?"

"For people like us, in positions of trust and authority, we would have been eligible for death."

28 Jennifer Grey Mysteries

"So that was really what you risked."

"Of course. And we would do it again."

"And how did you do it?"

Natalya and Sergei looked at each other and then at the dozing Officer Bishop. Jennifer leaned over and turned the TV sound off.

Five

"This may make us sound crazy," Natalya began quietly in a delicate, thickly accented voice. "But trying to escape and dying for it would have been better than to go on living in the Soviet Union."

Sergei put an arm around her shoulder. "We had to believe that with all our hearts before we left for Canada, because once we got on that plane, we had no alternative plan."

The young couple told Jennifer how they had all but scripted their lines and actions but, of course, weren't foolish enough to put anything in writing. The plan was that Natalya would act impetuous again in the airport, make everyone wait by being late from shopping, and act frivolous. She pushed it to the point where she was lectured by the group leader.

Once in the air, Sergei went to the leader and recommended that Natalya be returned to the Soviet Union immediately upon their landing in Montreal. "The leader told me he had dealt forthrightly with her and that her discipline was not my concern unless I wanted the responsibility. Which, of course, was just what we wanted."

"Why?"

"Child psychology," Natalya said carefully, smiling.

Sergei explained. "Soviet administrators are insecure. They do not like being told what to do by subordinates. They will often do the opposite of what they think you want. We believe it is because they must obey the party and their many superiors, so they protect the little authority they *have* been charged with."

"So how did it help you that the group leader was upset with Natalya, but not upset enough to make her return to the Soviet Union?"

"Well, she was one of the best tour guides, and he knew it. She had never misbehaved while leading a tour in Russia. She was only disruptive when the whole group was together. The leader scolded her for not being serious and responsible enough. She was also warned that she would never get to go on another trip like this one. We thought that was funny, because we knew she would either wind up in America or Siberia anyway."

"Why run the risk that the leader might take you up on your suggestion and send her back?"

29

30 Jennifer Grey Mysteries

"Ah, it was really no risk," Sergei said. "I didn't present it as a request. I presented it as a *demand*, I insisted that she be sent back. That got me in trouble, and I wound up getting lectured too."

"And that was part of your plan?"

"Yes," Natalya said. "Remember child psychology. What do you think our leader planned to do?"

"Tell me."

"He decided to fix us both by making some switches. He put me in Sergei's group so Sergei would be responsible for me and for six others. He knew we hated each other. He wanted to make me behave, and he wanted to get back at Sergei for telling him what to do. He also knew that Sergei would be particularly strict with me, and that would keep me in line."

"Pretty crafty."

Sergei smiled. "We thought so. We had been working on the plan for two years. I can't tell you the number of times we rehearsed our lines, our little speeches to the group leader. He was a very nervous, very stern fellow. He had people to report to, and he had a very sensitive job. Our task in Montreal was to see how Canadian guides handled the many tourists in so many languages. The city itself has two languages you know, French and English. Well, of course, you know. Excuse me."

Jennifer smiled at him. "So you landed in Montreal."

"Yes, and Natalya was wonderful! She pouted, she argued, she giggled, she took other girls running here and there."

"And you?"

"I was cross with her, warning her, threatening her, staying close and keeping an eye on her. I also reported her to the group leader. I was so earnest that he almost took charge of her himself. That was the scariest part, until we actually made our break."

"What would you have done if he had taken charge of her?"

They looked at each other and shrugged. "It simply couldn't happen, that's all. He had too much on his mind. He was frustrated, and we were convincing, but he just looked me deep in the eyes and pointed at me and said, 'You, Baranov, will answer for Danilin. You will see that she behaves in Canada and that she is delivered safely back to the Soviet Union with us. We will deal with her there, and with you, sir, if you do not succeed. We will not be embarrassed. She is *your* problem.'"

"He played right into your hands."

"Right. We spent several days in Montreal, visiting the site where Russian athletes had performed at the 1976 Olympic Games. We toured

The Calling 31

the city and studied how the guides handled us and the English and French speaking tourists."

"It must have been fun."

"It was horrible," Natalya said. "We could not help but feel pride in the history of our athletes, and the Canadians had obviously been cautioned not to criticize us or our country or government. They were wonderful to us, and it was difficult for both Sergei and me to maintain our hatred for Soviet life, which we needed to carry out our plan."

"You mean you were actually getting a new view of your home country?"

"Yes!" Sergei said. "But we had to keep reminding ourselves that we knew the truth. Each of us feared the other was wavering, and it was difficult not to become emotional at hearing our national anthem every night at various events."

"But we could not talk together," Natalya said. "We could have given great encouragement to each other, but we could not be seen together unless we argued."

"Then you escaped from where? Montreal?"

"No, no," Sergei said. "We wanted to wait until the last day when the group would be heading home and could not wait around to see if we were located. The trip was two weeks. We spent most of the first week in Montreal, then traveled by bus to Ottawa and on to Toronto."

"So Toronto was your spot."

"Right. And as we drew closer and closer, we became more and more nervous. It was very draining. We did not sleep well. We were irritable. I was trying to act irritated with Natalya, yet I was truly irritated with everyone else. I heard them talking among themselves about how Canada was not really that impressive, and how the people didn't seem happy, and how they were really much happier and freer and more productive in Russia. They were lying to themselves! I wanted to stand and shout at them and show them how wrong they were. I wanted to remind them of the oppression, the sadness, the frustration. I know that with a few well-placed questions I could have started many of them thinking about doing what we were planning, but it was not worth the risk. I had never done it before, and I would not start now. Who knew how many KGB might be among our group?"

Sergei had become emotional and stopped to collect himself. Natalya stroked his arm. "People who lead uprisings," she said, "who stir up the passions of others, who urge them to look honestly about themselves and decide if they are totally free in Russia—those people are gone. Reassigned. Transferred. Moved."

32 Jennifer Grey Mysteries

"Siberia," Sergei said. "Many people joke about it, even in Russia. But it is not funny."

"I was careful as we got into Ottawa," Natalya said. "I did not want anyone thinking that I was unhappy with the Soviet Union. I just wanted the reputation of being flighty and of not liking this beast, Sergei Baranov. If I grew moody and sullen and disrespectfiul of *all* authority, I would have been watched even more closely."

"So when the guides got into discussions comparing Canada and the USSR, Natalya argued passionately for Russia. It was very difficult for me, because I wondered if she was trying to tell me that she had changed her mind."

"It was difficult for me too," Natalya said. "Because I was being so deceitful. I wanted to be a behavior problem so they would keep Sergei watching me. But I did not want to be thought of as a traitor, or we would have never had the chance to escape."

They waited, they told Jennifer, until the last day the group was to be in Canada. The group was to fly out of Toronto early in the evening. Each small group was free from before lunch until they had to be back on the bus at five-thirty for the ride to the airport.

"I split my group into four pairs," Sergei said, "just to show them I trusted them. They loved it. They were excited and kept asking, 'Really? Can we really split up and meet back together later?' I told them they could, but that each pair had to stay together. I also told them where I'd be, because that was part of Natalya's and my plan."

"The first thing I did," Natalya said, "was to find out what my partner, Raisa, wanted most to see and do. First, she was hungry. Then she wanted to see the Royal Ontario Museum. That was the best news I'd heard all day. We picked up some brochures that told us how to get to the museum, and we decided to walk. I noticed on the map that there was a shopping mall before the restaurant and also a movie theatre several blocks before the museum. It couldn't have been better."

Natalya told Jennifer that she first talked excitedly to Raisa about their afternoon and how they should find a cute restaurant and take their time eating, then stroll to the museum and spend the rest of the afternoon there.

"Raisa was very excited, and I hated to spoil her fun, but she was simply a pawn in our plan."

"What did you do?"

"Well, I kept talking about food and how we might like some more of the Western cuisine we had enjoyed in Canada so far. I could tell she was really getting hungry, and we located a little place on our map that we decided would be perfect. But I walked very slowly and window shopped for about one hour.

"When we finally got to the shopping mall, a couple of blocks from the restaurant and about half a kilometer from the museum, I begged Raisa to let me walk through the mall. She started getting irritated with me, but I insisted, and she finally followed me through the mall, urging me along. 'I'm hungry, Natalya,' she kept saying. She would have made me hungry, too, if I hadn't been so nervous.

"Finally, Raisa pleaded with me to come eat with her. I told her to go on ahead. She said she did not want to go alone, so I said, 'Well, just a few more minutes then.' Twenty minutes later she was almost in tears and threatened to tell Sergei about me. I told her to go ahead. She waited another ten minutes or so, then told me she was going to tell him. She left. But I did not believe her. I knew she would give me one chance more. I just kept browsing through clothing, and sure enough, she returned. 'Are you coming, Natalya?' she asked timidly. I was cruel to her. I said, 'No, little Raisa. I thought you were going to get me in trouble with Baranov, so I decided to just stay here and wait for him to come and yell at me.'

" 'Come on, Natalya!' she said. And I said, 'No! You go on. I'm happy to stay here shopping.' When she left that time, I knew she was gone for good. So I quickly spent almost two hundred dollars that I changed into Canadian money at the hotel. I bought clothes and backpacks for Sergei and me, and on the way out of the mall, I bought sausages and bread."

"So, did Raisa get to you, Sergei?"

"Oh, yes! I had told everyone where I'd be with Alexsander. He was quite a lover of trains so we were spending a lot of time at the station. Actually I was expecting Raisa much sooner, and as Alexsander and I sat in the depot restaurant, I was afraid he would notice that I was preoccupied or looking over his shoulder or something.

"But when Raisa finally arrived, I looked genuinely surprised and upset over how she described Natalya's behavior. 'She just wants to shop, shop, shop!' Raisa complained. I suggested that she ask her to compromise and please hurry to lunch and then to the museum. I didn't want to be too quick to offer to trade partners. Raisa assured me that she had tried everything and that Natalya was just being impossible. Inside, I was cheering for her great job and hoping she was getting everything arranged.

"'Can't you go talk to her, Sergei?' Raisa asked. 'It's your responsibility, and I can't get through to her.' I asked her where Natalya was, and she showed me on the map. Just to be certain they would suspect nothing, I said, 'Alex, old friend, do this for me, will you? Run and tell this spoiled girl that she has to go with Raisa, and that I said so.'

34   Jennifer Grey Mysteries

"I was so relieved when he said, 'Forget it, Sergei! She's *your* problem!'
I said, 'Well, then, would you mind switching partners? I'll go find Natalya
and make her behave, and you let Raisa finish my lunch here and then take
her to the museum.' He said he'd already seen enough trains for one day,
and he readily agreed."

"Which we knew he would," Natalya said, smiling. "It was the plan all
along. We could see they had eyes for each other, but they had not
declared themselves yet. It was the whole reason for the original pairings."

"Yes," Sergei said, "and to make sure they didn't follow too soon and
find us heading another direction, I ordered another sandwich for Raisa.
But as I was leaving the restaurant I went back to Alexsander and said,
'Are you sure you won't do this for me, Alex? I'll owe you one.' He waved
me away, and I stalked out with an angry look. 'I'll see you on the bus at
five-thirty,' I said. By the time I was out the door and looked back, they
were already smiling and talking."

Natalya turned to lie on her stomach and rest on her elbows, facing
Jennifer. "By now I was done with my shopping and running toward our
meeting place, the bus station. I was lugging two full backpacks, but I was
so excited I hardly noticed. I bought two tickets to Windsor and then ran
into the washroom where I changed into my Western-style clothes. I sat on
a bench pretending to read an American novel with my backpacks next to
me, hoping I looked like a Canadian."

"And she did," Sergei said. "I almost ran right past her. I knew she
would be there, but the look was so total, the boots, the jeans, the blouse,
the jacket. She had even worked with her hair, tied it back or something.
But she couldn't hide her tininess or her beauty. I recognized her soon. She
tossed me my backpack, and I went and changed. We looked like twins."
He laughed. "Except for our height, of course, and the colors of our
backpacks."

"That's when we changed our plan slightly," Natalya said. "We were
going to change nothing, but we decided that if someone got suspicious
and we were reported missing, they would look in bus and train stations
and taxi companies and ask if a couple of our description had been seen.
We decided to travel separately. On the same bus, I mean, but not
together."

"We worried," Sergei said, "that someone would think we looked a lot
alike because of our clothes, but Natalya had done such a good job of
buying what was popular that we just looked like everyone else. She'd had
to memorize my sizes, of course, because if she'd ever been found with
them written down, it might have given us away."

The Calling

"So, you took the bus from Toronto to Windsor, but you didn't sit together?"

"No, and it was difficult," Sergei said. "We almost felt free, but we didn't want to defect in Canada while our group was still there. The KGB has a way of talking authorities into forcing you to at least talk with them. Then they forge a confession and drag you back to your group, announcing that you had your fun and now you're changing your mind."

"So we listened carefully to the conversations around us," Natalya said. "And we tried very hard to sound Canadian, or American, if we were ever asked any questions."

"Did you know the difference between Canadian and American accents?"

"Not really, because we didn't know if the people talking were one or the other," Natalya said. "The only thing Sergei wanted us to learn to say as clearly as possible and without giving away our accents, was 'Canada. Yes. Pleasure. A few days.'"

"That was all?"

"I hoped so," Sergei said. "If they asked us anything else at the border, I didn't know what I'd do. I was afraid that by the time we got there, our bus in Toronto would have been waiting for us for about an hour, and the authorities would already be looking for us. When we got off the bus in Windsor we didn't see anything suspicious, so we took a cab to the border and walked together to one of the crossing stations, trying as hard as we knew how to look like Canadians."

Six

"The cab was easier," Sergei said, "because the driver didn't care who we were or where we were from or how we talked. All he cared about was where we were going and how much he could charge us for getting there."

"Sergei asked him to let us off a few blocks from the border station so it wouldn't look suspicious—I mean our taking a cab to the border and then walking across."

"So," Sergei continued, "we walked up to a station, feeling very self-conscious because we were the only ones in that line who were not in a car. But there were other lines that had people standing in them, so we knew it was all right. We picked the longest line so the guard would be in a hurry to move people through.

"When it was our turn, the guard asked, 'Traveling together?' I said, 'Yes,' and Natalya nodded. 'Born in Canada?' I said, Yes, again, and Natalya nodded. He looked directly at her. 'You too, honey?' he asked. She said, 'Yes,' just as plain as could be. 'How long in the U.S.?' he asked. 'A few days,' I said, trying to emphasize my uncertainty over the time to take his mind off any accent that might slip through. He looked away from us and was writing on a clipboard. 'Business or pleasure?' he continued, sounding bored. 'Pleasure,' I said. The best thing we did, I think, and Natalya was so good at this, was to pretend that we did this all the time. We acted as bored as he did, and we didn't look nervous or worried. 'Have a good time,' he said. I just nodded and smiled, and we walked across."

"Then we went straight to the American authorities," Natalya said. "Sergei told them, very proudly and in his best English—though no longer worrying about his accent—that we were Russian defectors from an Intourist delegation in Toronto and that we wanted political asylum."

"I also told them that we wanted to tell our story before the KGB came looking for us and trying to get us back. We wanted to ensure against any false confessions or crazy stories about our being undesirables or criminals."

"And how did the authorities treat you?"

Sergei smiled at Natalya. "Like dignitaries," she said. "They called in a lot of other people who greeted us like old, welcome friends. They fed us, interviewed us, assured us that we would be protected, and carefully

The Calling

37

searched our bags. They did ask a lot of questions about our status with the Soviet Union, any friends who might be following us, everywhere we had been, and what we had done since we had been in Canada, and lots of other things."

"They were simply trying to be sure that we were not bad people," Sergei said. "They were impressed with how much money we had; but we had been saving for many, many years. They were very curious about what we planned to do. We said we wanted to be married as soon as possible, and they said that we would at least have to have blood tests first and that there might be a little more processing and checking before we could settle somewhere. I had always wanted to come to Chicago, so we decided we'd come here. They told us we should stay there in Detroit for two or three days while they established that we were not being hunted down and while they saw that we were officially listed as defectors with the proper documents and testimony."

"I'll never forget the day that they told us we were free to go and encouraged us to take a bus to Chicago," Natalya said. "They told us of safe, inexpensive places to stay."

"Sort of," Sergei said, laughing. "Places like this one. Not cheap. Not fancy, but not cheap."

"We sat next to each other on the bus from Detroit to Chicago, and we finally felt free. Scared, but free."

"What were you scared of? You must have thought the KGB had given up on you and that you were fairly safe."

"You never feel safe from the KGB, no matter how long you are away. Anything can happen. But we were most scared of our freedom."

"You'll have to explain that," Jennifer said, scribbling furiously and flipping pages to find blank ones. Officer Bishop's hands dangled at his sides, and his head had rolled to one side.

"With no restrictions," Sergei said, "we almost didn't know what to do. The authorities in Detroit had started the paper work on naturalization so we can someday become citizens. We had temporary work permits so we could get work and be paid. But we realized that when we got into Chicago and found a cheap apartment, all we knew to do then was to try to get married and find work. No one would tell us where to go or not go. No one would tell us what we could do or not do. Few requirements. Just freedom. True freedom. To do what you want, when you want, how you want. We had lost the security of oppression. That sounds crazy, doesn't it?"

"No. I see what you mean. But didn't it also excite you?"

"In a way, yes," Sergei said. "But in another way, it will take a lot of getting used to. It was all we talked about on the bus from Detroit, and that

38   Jennifer Grey Mysteries

was a long ride. We decided not to circulate each time the bus stopped.
Others were getting snacks or buying souvenirs, but we either stayed on
the bus or strolled near it. We still didn't want to take any chances. We
decided that we wouldn't feel totally free until we were safely in Chicago."

"It was such a strange feeling," Natalya said. "To be on a bus and going
to a big city, and the only people who knew were the authorities in
Detroit, and with them it was OK. They had advised us where to stay and
what to do, but they hadn't commanded us. There were a few things we
were required to do, yes, like getting the proper permits and starting our
citizenship process, but you see, after that we could do what we wanted.
Literally, do what we wanted." She looked above Jennifer's head, as if into
a limitless horizon.

"You see why it makes such an impact on us?" Sergei asked. Jennifer
nodded. "It's almost as if we have so many things to choose from we don't
know where to begin. We decided that when we got to Chicago, we would
stay in a hotel for one night and eat there. We understand that at some of
the big hotels, like on Michigan Avenue—is that right—?" Jennifer
nodded again. "Yes, that the restaurants at the hotels are as fancy as any.
We wanted a big American meal and a fancy hotel room. They might even
serve the meal in the room, no?"

Jennifer smiled. "Yes," she said, "and in the morning you would have a
bill you wouldn't believe."

"How much, in American dollars?"

"Depends on what you had to eat and how nice your room was."

"Say a regular room and a big dinner for two."

"Well over one hundred dollars; maybe two hundred."

"Oh, no!" Natalya said. "We would have been in for a surprise! We have
only six hundred American dollars left."

"And you'd better guard that six hundred with your lives because you"ll
need most of it for a deposit on your apartment. And then you'll have to
find work as quickly as possible so you'll have money to live on."

"Sergei can teach history, and I can teach Americans to speak Russian."

"Do you both have degrees?"

"Not actually degrees, but we were both honor students at university and
can probably pass whatever test is necessary to teach here."

"Perhaps. And I'm guessing that some colleges here would love to have
the real thing teaching their students, degrees or not. You may have to
finish your education to get far here though."

"The real thing?"

"I just meant native Russians, who not only speak the language and
know the history, but who have also lived there all their lives. And you're
both so fluent, really."

The Calling

"Sergei is better at speaking English than I," Natalya said. "But I will catch up when I've been here long enough."

"You shouldn't have any trouble here. Nothing will be as frightening for you as what you have already come through."

Sergei stood and walked to the window, leaning back against the wall next to it. "That's the problem," he said quietly so as not to awaken Fred Bishop. "We haven't come through it yet. You can't imagine how scared we were when we stood to get off the bus in Chicago and saw your Jim and Officer Bishop standing at the door."

"Did you know they were policemen? They were in plain clothes, weren't they?"

"Yes, but when two serious-looking men are standing one on either side of the door and carefully peering into the face of every passenger, it can mean only one thing."

"Sergei was worried," Natalya said, "but I couldn't see the men over the crowd in the bus. I kept telling him that we were not in the Soviet Union anymore and that unless the men looked like Russian KGB, we had nothing to worry about."

"But when they spotted me," Sergei said, "I could see it in their eyes, and I knew they were talking to each other without looking at each other, which is always a sign. They were saying something like, 'That's him. Where is she? There she is.' I wanted to run out through the back, but there was no exit. And there were too many people behind us. Then I thought about pushing the people in front of us into the two men and trying to just break away through the crowd and see if we could escape."

"In fact," Natalya said, "Sergei was quite upset with himself. Here he had kept his head through the toughest part of our plan, and now he was giving himself away by looking all around and appearing scared."

"Oh, I definitely confirmed our identity in their minds, because I looked at them as if I knew they were looking for us. There was no turning back now, and I was terribly frustrated. If I could have thought ahead a little better, I would have tried to fake my best English and act upset that anyone was trying to detain us. But I had lost my composure, and unless I wanted to create a terrible scene, I knew we'd been caught."

"Did you know they were Americans?"

"Oh, yes. I don't think I ever thought they were Russian. I don't know why. I can tell the difference, I guess. I just didn't think about it. When we stepped off the bus, Officer Bishop identified himself as the Chicago Police and said, 'You're coming with us.' I asked, 'What've we done?' and noticed that Jim—of course, I didn't know his name yet—was giving his partner a dirty look. He said to us, 'If you are Sergei Baranov and Natalya Danilin, we'd like you to come with us for your own protection.' "

40 Jennifer Grey Mysteries

"Did that put you at ease?"

"Not entirely, but I certainly could tell that Officer Purcell meant us no harm. I couldn't understand the other one's attitude. It was as if we were being arrested. We were glad that Officer Purcell took over as soon as we got past the crowd and into a little office in the bus station.

"Jim told us who he was and showed us his badge. He told us that federal officials in Detroit had reason to believe we were being followed by KGB, and he and his partner had been assigned to protect us until we had a chance to decide whether we wanted to talk to Soviet authorities."

"Sergei immediately told them that we had decided that a long time ago," Natalya said, "and that he could be sure that we wanted no contact whatever with KGB. He asked how we could be protected from them, and Officer Purcell explained the plan."

"Which is?"

"We would be brought here and protected until federal authorities had time to negotiate with any Soviet officials. We knew what the KGB would do. They would represent themselves as diplomats and try to strong-arm the U.S. into letting them talk with us. They'll make all kinds of threats and try to make it appear as if we have been kidnapped or brainwashed or held against our wills. Our not wanting to talk to them would only make it appear that they were right, but we absolutely refuse to do it anyway."

"Are you afraid of them?"

"Absolutely! It would not be beyond the scope of the KGB to drug us while we are talking with them. They could harm us, take us back, make up stories about us. More than likely, they would come from a private meeting with us with a signed confession and also a written request that we not be subjected to any more harassment from U.S. authorities. They would insist that no one from the U.S. be allowed to talk with us again and make it appear, and convincingly so, that we had requested that ourselves. Then we would be lost. Siberia, or worse."

"Would U.S. authorities stand for that?"

"What recourse would they have? They'd have to embarrass their Soviet contacts and call them liars. By that time, we would be threatened with harm to our families if we did speak to U.S. officials. No, Miss Grey, once we fall into the hands of KGB, or however they represent themselves here, we're as good as back in Russia."

Jennifer took a deep breath and looked at the two young defectors. "Everything we've said here has been on-the-record, except for what you specifically asked me not to print, am I right?"

"Right," Natalya said. "The truth is our best defense. Sergei has been saying that for years."

The Calling

"Wait," Sergei said, looking deeply troubled. "If it is not too late, and if you are indeed allowing us the freedom to request this, I wish that you would not write what I said about the KGB threatening our families."

"It's pretty powerful stuff, Sergei."

"I know," he said. "And true too. And I know that truth can only help us. But I would hate to give the KGB any ideas. If the word came out of Russia that our families were suffering for our freedom, I don't know if I could live with it."

"There is already much pain involved with our families," Natalya said, and her voice quavered. "We may never have contact with them again, even indirectly."

"They can't write to you? You can't get your address to them somehow? Won't they try to write to you through the international news agencies?"

"No, no!" Sergei said, waving. "They could if they wished, but all mail going in or out from them or to them will now be subject to investigation. But more important, they will have disowned us. In their minds, we will no longer exist. Everyone in Russia is subject to the oppression, but leaving is unforgivable. They will never want to think about us again."

"In their minds, perhaps," Jennifer said. "But do you really believe you will leave their hearts?"

Sergei and Natalya looked at the floor, and then at each other. Natalya began to weep. "I love them," she said.

Sergei stood straighter and turned his back to Jennifer and Natalya, pretending to look out the window through the side of the curtain. Soon his head dropped and he rubbed his eyes with his hand.

"If by any chance anything you write would find its way into Russia," he said with difficulty, "it would maybe be good for us to tell how we feel about our parents, whether they accept or believe it or not. The most difficult thing about leaving was knowing that we were losing them forever. They had nothing to do with our escape, and they had no knowledge of it. Whatever they hear from whatever source, they should believe only what we say to you. My parents hardly know Natalya's parents, and they might each try to blame the child of the other. But we share whatever blame there is to share. Our love and our need for freedom—true freedom—forced us to follow our consciences. You may write that."

Seven

This time, Jennifer and Natalya's embrace was not awkward. Jennifer got the impression that Natalya understood her intentions and accepted her support, her best wishes, her welcome to a new homeland.

Sergei, in what Jennifer thought was a rather transparent attempt to avoid an embarrassing situation, approached Jennifer and offered her his hand, which she gripped warmly. "Will we get to see what you're going to put in the paper before it appears?" he asked.

"No," she said quickly. "That's a policy of the paper and of the reporters too. You'll have to trust me."

"How do we know we can?"

"You don't. You tell me tomorrow, after you've seen it, whether I'm trustworthy or not. And if I am, I'd like to ask you not to contact any other reporters until you come out of hiding."

"You want an exclusive," Sergei said, smiling.

"You're well read," Jennifer said.

"What if other reporters contact us?"

"They won't. I won't give away where you are. I'd have the Chicago Police Department, not to mention untold federal agencies, down on my neck. They want this publicity for you; it makes their jobs easier. Giving away your hideout would only make it more difficult."

"We want the publicity too," Sergei said. "That's why we are forced to trust you, even though it goes against everything I have learned in life."

"But you learned your suspicion in the Soviet Union," Jennifer said.

Sergei nodded. Natalya spoke. "Also, Sergei, you have always been a good judge of character. That's why you didn't care so much for him"— she pointed at Bishop—"from the beginning, but you like Mr. Purcell. And his girlfriend is the same. Can't you tell?"

"Of course, I can," Sergei said. "But Miss Grey also understands my fears. Don't you?"

"I do," she said. "And I'm eager to prove my trustworthiness to you. I'll find out from Jim if I can deliver the paper to you tomorrow myself. By

The Calling   43

then, they'll probably have come up with a rotation of officers to stay with you, one every eight hours.

"But now," Jennifer said, "I have to get to the office. I normally write my Sunday column before noon on Saturday, even though my deadline is four P.M. My boss will probably be looking for me when he finds out I'm not in yet."

As she zipped up her coat and unlatched the chain lock, Bishop stirred. When she opened the door and the sub-zero wind blew in, he stood quickly, his hand on the revolver at his hip. "Oh, you leavin, Jenn?" he asked. "I musta dozed off there a minute."

Jennifer was right. Leo Stanton, her boss, was on the phone when she arrived, calling his various contacts among her colleagues, asking if they had seen her. "Oh, here she is now," he said. "Sorry to bother you."

Leo stood. He was dressed the way he might be during the week, except today there was no tie or jacket. But the woolen slacks, the Oxford broadcloth shirt, the cardigan, the ever-present unlit cigar, the half-glasses pushed up to his forehead, they were all there. He cursed under his breath. "Where you been, girl?" he asked. "You know I always call Saturday mornings to see what you've cooked up for Sunday."

"I know, Leo, and I'm sorry. But this one is worth it."

"It'd better be. I'm only in here because you weren't. You know I hate to come in on Saturdays."

"I would have called you in anyway," she said, producing her dog-eared notebook. "You won't believe I got this from the cops."

"I'd believe anything. Just tell me you didn't get it from Jim."

She looked up at him with one eye shut. "Well, I did, but it's all right. Trust me."

"*Trust you?* You're not on the police beat anymore, Jennifer. We're talkin' front-page feature column stuff. It's not often the police blotter has the grist for that. You realize you're competing with probably the most famous local columnist in the country in this town."

"No, Leo, really? You mean there's another columnist in this town? How would I know that? I never read the papers!"

"All right, I'm sorry. Get on with it. What've you got, and how am I gonna keep city hall off my back if it's obvious you got this from Jim?"

"It was the brass's idea, Leo. Now sit down, and let me give it to you."

He pointed to a chair and then came around and sat on the corner of his desk facing her. He let his head fall back, and he rubbed his eyes with the tips of his fingers. The pressure loosened the grip of his glasses on his forehead, and when he took his hands away and looked down at her, his

44   Jennifer Grey Mysteries

glasses slid down and settled on the end of his nose. He stared at her over the top.

Within minutes, Jennifer had him pacing his office. "Dynamite," he said over and over. "It's great! How much space will you need?"

"I can go as long or as short as you want, Leo, but there's a lot here. It's going to take me more than an hour to bang it out if I start right now while it's still fresh in my mind."

He called the production room to check on the first two pages of the Sunday edition. He was assured that a hole had been left for Jennifer Grey's column.

"I don't care about that," he said. "I need room for about twice her normal column on page one and about half of page two for a sidebar and the continuation of the column. Yes, the column will be that long. Send me up a proof of what one and two look like right now, and I'll tell you what can be moved or killed."

Leo turned to Jennifer. "Better get started."

She dumped her things on a side chair in her office and turned on her video display terminal. She began her column:

A young Russian couple defecting from the Soviet Union have chosen Chicago as their new home. But if the KGB has its way, they could be living—or dying—in Siberia by the end of next week.

While Jennifer was working, Leo assigned a reporter to write a sidebar for page two, to run alongside the continuation of Jennifer's page one column. The sidebar would tell of some of the more celebrated defections from the USSR, including Oleg and Irina Chulkov and several dancers and athletes.

Little more than an hour later, Leo was thrilled with Jennifer's column. "We'll follow it up every day next week with more quotes from them, the progress of negotiations with the Soviets, the whole bit. You have access to them?"

"Sure."

"I can't think of better columns for next week," he said. "Can you?"

Jennifer got no answer on the phone at Jim's, so she decided to go to her own place and get some rest, hoping to call him at Rasto's during his shift. But when she got home, her own phone was ringing. It was Jim.

"I was hoping to get to the mortgage company today before I have to go back on duty," he said.

"The mortgage company? Aren't we all set with the house? I thought everything was signed and all we have to do is close next month."

The Calling

"But, Jennifer, if we're not going to even be in the Chicago area, we need to bail out of this house deal as soon as we can."

Jennifer was silent. It wasn't that they hadn't discussed it. She knew his feelings, his leanings, his convictions. But she hadn't conceded that it was all going to happen just the way he said. She had never agreed to quit her job or help put him through Bible school, seminary, or missionary training.

"Do I have any input on this at all?" she asked finally, weakly.

"Sure, yes, of course you do, Jennifer. But you know how it's probably going to go if the Lord wants us to do this. Don't you think we should put the brakes on for this deal and if things change, we can look for another home?"

"Jim, we can't talk about this over the phone. I felt God led us to that house. He was in that too, you know. You said so yourself. It was a good deal, a good location, the right timing. Were we wrong about His leading us there?"

"Maybe it was a test, Jenn. He wanted to get us excited about that and then see if we were willing to give it up for Him."

That didn't sound like the God of order that Jennifer worshiped. Hers wasn't a God of games and tests. But when Jim was excited about something, convinced about something, wrapped up in something, there was no talking him out of it.

"Jim, I really am not prepared to take this step just now. I think we have time to wait on the house deal, and if God confirms that this is what He wants for us, He'll provide the time to get out of the arrangement. Don't you agree?"

"Jenn, what more does He have to do to show us this is what He wants for us?"

She paused, seething. She didn't want to fly off the handle, but she feared the day was going to come when she would have to either blow up at Jim or push him to blow up at her. "He has to tell *me*," she said.

"Jennifer! He's telling you through *me*! That's how God works with husbands and wives."

"We're *not* husband and wife, Jim!" she said, knowing how it sounded and wishing she hadn't had to say it. Finally, she had elicited nothing from him but silence. It was the best part of the conversation from her perspective.

"Apparently, we *do* need to talk face-to-face," he said. "And soon."

"That would be good, Jim."

"Oh, Jennifer, don't you see how this assignment of protecting Sergei and Natalya is just further affirmation that God wants me in missionary

46 Jennifer Grey Mysteries

work? It's as if He brought someone from overseas into my life just to show me the need and the potential and how I could serve Him so much better if I am willing to go wherever He sends me."

"I can see how you might feel that way, especially after hearing the sermons we heard at church last week."

"But you think I'm putting two and two together and getting five."

"I just don't want to discuss it by phone, Jim. This may be the most important thing we ever talk about."

"*May* be? What could be more important?"

"Nothing, I know. And you'll wait on the mortgage thing?"

"I can't do anything without you on that anyway."

"I appreciate that, Jim."

Immediately after Jennifer hung up, she dialed her parents' home in Rockford, Illinois. "Dad, I was wondering if you and Mom might be able to visit me tonight."

"Something wrong?"

"Oh, not really. I just need someone to talk to."

"Well, your mother can't come. She's on some ladies' retreat until late Sunday afternoon. I guess I could make it, unless you thought you could come this way."

"I wish I could, Dad, but I'm on a story that requires I stay around here if at all possible. Does the *Morning Star* still carry my column?"

"Are you kidding? They always identify you as 'Rockford's own Jennifer Knight Grey.'"

"Well, by tomorrow morning you'll know about the big story if you stay there and wait for the *Star*. But if you come in time for dinner tonight, I'll give you a sneak preview."

"I can't pass that up. But Jenny, listen—no cooking for me tonight. You couldn't make me happier than to let me take you out, just the two of us, hear?"

"Are you sure?"

"Never surer. Please let me do this. After next month I may never get to do it again. I'll always have that husband of yours along. And you know I think he's the greatest, but—"

"He's not my husband yet, Dad."

"You know what I meant."

"Yeah, I know. When can I expect you?"

"Well, I'll have to get gussied up a bit here, but I'll leave within the hour. Then give me another hour and a half."

"Sounds good. You may have to wake me with the doorbell or call when you get here. I've been up since about two this morning."

The Calling

"Good grief, Jenn. Are you sure you're up to this?"

"Up to it? I *need* it, Dad. See you soon."

Jennifer showered and laid out her clothes for the evening, then slept soundly for a little more than an hour. She was awakened by the phone. She was groggy, and she couldn't believe her father could be there already.

"Hello?"

"Jenn, it's Jim. We may have a problem at Rasto's. I just wanted you to know. I called to see how Fred was doing and to tell him I was going to be there a little before seven, but I'm getting no answer."

"Uh, maybe he took them out for dinner," Jennifer suggested, still trying to clear her head.

"No, he knows better than that. Something's happened. We're sending a car over there."

"Did you talk to the people at the desk?"

"At Rasto's?"

"Yeah."

"Well, we kinda didn't want them to know we had three or four people in the room. When we checked in, we just told 'em there would be two of us."

"They could at least tell you if anyone was there when they cleaned up the room."

"That's just it. To make sure not even the maids knew how many people were there, we hung the do not disturb sign on the doorknob and called the office to tell them not to bother with cleaning the room today."

"Somebody could at least tell you if Fred's car is still there."

"We'll know soon enough. I'm going over there too."

"You know, Jim," Jennifer said, finally sitting up and thinking more clearly, "Fred was sleeping most of the morning and into the early afternoon, from the time I started interviewing Sergei and Natalya to the time I left."

"He was sleeping when you left?"

"He woke up just as I was going out the door. And he had been inappropriate with both Natalya and me earlier."

"You're kidding!"

"That surprises you?"

"Well, you're just talking about what he says, aren't you, Jennifer? I mean he was just the same old Fred, right? He didn't try anything, did he?"

"No, but I wouldn't put it past him. He's really quite crude."

"You sound like his first wife."

"Thanks."

"No, you know. I mean, she always said that about him."

"Didn't the second one too?"

"Sure. Still does. He knows his shortcomings, but I don't think he means any of it. He's harmless."

"I hope so."

"I'm sure of it," Jim said. "I just hope he's safe."

Jennifer wasn't sure she cared about Fred Bishop's welfare. She knew she should. But she was really worried about her new young friends, and she hoped Fred's irresponsibility had not cost them their freedom. Or their lives.

Eight

Jennifer felt so whipped, so dead tired, that she wished she could just lie back down, roll over, and tune out again. But she knew she had to call Leo. Of course, he wasn't still at the *Day* offices.

"Leo, I'm so sorry to have to call you at home."

"Hey, no problem, as long as you're not gonna tell me that the young aliens are phonies or criminals or something."

"None of the above. But they *are* missing."

"No."

"Yup. At least Jim can't get an answer at their hotel room. He's on his way there now. He'll probably be calling me with whatever they find."

"I know this sounds morbid, Jennifer, but it's almost more difficult for us if they find nothing."

"For the paper you mean."

"Yeah. I mean if they find KGB or foul play or whatever, at least we'll know what's going on. But what if someone has simply messed up, the cop maybe?"

"Entirely likely, but I'm worried."

"I can imagine. But if they just don't know where the cop or the other two have gone, we can hardly mention it in the later editions tomorrow."

"Too late to insert something in the column now to say that they're already missing?"

"Oh, yeah, way too late. They're rolling with the first edition right now, Jenn. I mean if we knew for sure they were dead or kidnapped or something, then we might just try stopping the run, but nothing short of that."

"Well, I'm sorry to disappoint you, Leo."

"Jennifer, you know I'm just being realistic. We just don't have enough here yet to hold the run, do you think?"

"I suppose not, but to me that's good news."

"Well, of course it is. You stay on top of it now, you hear? Because as soon as we know anything definite, we'll want to adjust for the later editions for tomorrow. You have a schedule of the press times?"

"Yeah, around here somewhere."

50 Jennifer Grey Mysteries

"I just can't see putting something in—not even in the second run—that says that they might be missing. We just don't know that. I agree it's scary and there's no reason they're not getting an answer at the motel room, but it doesn't tell us anything. It could be a phone problem. It could be they've decided not to answer. They could be out to dinner, anything."

"They're not supposed to be out to dinner."

"I know, but that's what I mean about the cop maybe messing up. If we go to press with your great column *and* this dramatic business that they've only been in town a few hours and they're missing already, and later we have to say, 'Oh, they were just at dinner with a cop who blew it,' we're gonna be the laughingstock."

"I know. I'll stay on it, Leo, but I need some sleep. I've been up since two, you know."

"Get what you can while you can," he said. "You'll want to stay as fresh as possible for this one. Let me know as soon as you have something solid."

A few minutes later, when Jennifer realized that she was indeed falling asleep again, she felt guilty. She had a foreboding sense of danger about what might have happened to Sergei and Natalya, yet she was going to be able to sleep in spite of it. That, she knew, was real fatigue.

When Jennifer awoke an hour and a half later to the ringing of her doorbell, she threw on her robe and padded out to look through the peephole. "Come in, Dad," she said, opening the door.

The big, white-haired man embraced her and held the back of her head in his massive hand. "I'll be right with you," she said. "I've got to make a couple of calls first."

"You usually do," he said, smiling, unbuttoning his trench coat and his suit coat and vest before settling down on the couch. "That's why I made the reservations for a half-hour from now, even though we're just ten minutes away."

"Where're we goin'?" she called out from the bedroom.

"Ritz Carlton sound all right?" he asked.

"The Ritz? Are you serious?"

" 'Course! Nothin' but the best for my girl."

"You didn't have to do that!"

"But you never would've forgiven me if I hadn't."

Jennifer got no answer at Jim's. Nor at Rasto's room 58. Neither Jim nor Fred Bishop could be located by their precinct dispatcher. "Is Captain Bram in?" she asked.

"Matter of fact, he is, Mrs. Grey. How'd you know that?"

The Calling

"Just lucky, I guess."

"Yes, Jennifer, this is Captain Bram. It's been a long time."

"Yes, it has, Norman. Good to talk to you again. Congratulations on your promotion. I appreciated your thinking of me on this defection case. Of course, you know why I'm calling."

"I do, and I'm afraid we know nothing. Jim and a couple of other men from here should be at Rasto's now, but we're getting no answer by phone or radio. I'll have Jim call you as soon as I hear anything, all right?"

"That would be fine. Could you tell him that if I'm not at home, I'll be at the Ritz Carlton. In the restaurant."

"Oh. A date, huh? Ha! Have a good time."

"It's with my father, Norm."

"I figured as much. I'll have him call you, Jennifer. And I'm looking forward to your column tomorrow."

"Thanks. I'm looking forward to finding Sergei and Natalya."

"Me too."

George Knight didn't act like an out-of-towner. He'd had a successful business for many years before retirement, and he had traveled all over the country. He had been successful. "Not successful enough to retire to some sunny climate," he always said, "after putting a son and two daughters through college. But successful enough."

He wasn't awed by the Ritz. He slipped the maitre d' a few dollars for a very secluded table with a lovely view. "She may be getting a phone call," he told the man. "Will she be able to take it at the table?"

"Certainly, Mr. Knight."

"Her name is Jennifer Grey."

"Yes, sir. I know."

"Oh, ho," he whispered as they sat down. "He knows it! Did you set that up? Sort of like having yourself paged at the airport!"

She laughed.

They studied the menu for a few minutes. "Say," Mr. Knight said, "since this was your idea and you're planning on seeking a little counsel from your old man tonight, how 'bout lettin' me play the chauvinist, just this once."

She gave him a puzzled look.

"You know, Jenny, I know how far we've come in society and all that, but you wouldn't think it demeaning if I ordered for both of us, would you? I mean, I won't presume to tell you what to eat; I want you to order anything you want. But let me tell the waiter for you, the way I was taught to do it."

52   Jennifer Grey Mysteries

"Sure, Dad, if you want to. It doesn't bother me. I want the oysters Rockefeller. And by the way, who taught you to do this?"

"My father."

"Really? I never would have thought Grandpa was learned in the ways of the world."

"Oh, yeah. Just before I went off to college, he and Ma took some of their savings and we dressed up, the four of us, and went to a fancy restaurant in Madison. The Exeter. Doesn't even exist anymore. Looked it up a few years ago. Parking lot."

"The four of you? Aunt Lucille too, you mean?"

"Yup. Lucy would've been in high school at the time, probably a sophomore. Yeah, a sophomore. Anyway, my pa said we were gonna pretend this was a double date, like I might have to endure in college— that was the way he put it. And he coached me for several nights at the dinner table before the big night."

"How'd it go?"

"Frustrating. Lucy was thrilled with it. Neither of us was allowed to date until we went off to college, so this was the closest she'd come to a night out with a guy. I was wanting to cut up and be silly, and that made Pa mad. Lucy was takin' the thing so seriously that she kept trying to tell me what to do and when and how to do it."

"Like what?"

"Letting her out of the car, opening the door, helping her with her coat, pulling out her chair. I'll never forget her sayin', 'George, if you even pretend to pull that chair out from under me, I'll scream!' And I laughed and laughed. But you know, it was kind of fun, and I did learn what I was supposed to do. It was only a few months later that I took a beautiful young blonde from Beloit out to dinner. Gal named Lillian."

Jennifer smiled at the mention of her mother's name. "Dad, since you're being chauvinistic tonight by your own admission, can I ask you how you treated Mom early in your marriage?"

After Mr. Knight had ordered and while they were having their appetizers, he tried to reconstruct the first year of the marriage, nearly forty years before.

He admitted, "There was a lot to get used to. For both of us. I guess I was the strong, silent type, or at least I wanted to be. And she wanted me to be too. In many ways, I think she found some security in letting me handle the things a man was supposed to handle. We've changed a lot over the years, but I recall that I made the big financial decisions, and she handled the checkbook. I decided who we would or would not have over to the house, but she served as hostess when they came. I think I saw the inequities in all of that long before the women's movement raised the issues. But I can't take the credit for having noticed it right off or all by myself."

"You mean Mom pointed some of those things out to you?"

"Oh, yes. See, one thing she wanted me to lead in that I ran from was the spiritual aspect. She had always seemed more devout than I was. I mean, I was a churchgoing man, and I was a believer. Even read my Bible and prayed a lot. I prayed before every meal, but that was the extent of my spiritual leadership in the home, 'cept I drove to church, of course."

Jennifer smiled. "How did that change? I always remember you as the spiritual leader."

"Yeah, well, by the time your memory would have kicked into gear, your Mom and me had it out about a lot of things."

"A fight?"

"Naw. Never. You know better than that. I worship the ground she walks on. I could no more have a fight with your mother than stay mad at you when you were a stubborn high schooler with the temper of a sailor."

"So how did you have it out?"

"She just told me that there were some things she had to know, some things we had to get straight, for her own peace of mind. Boy, I wish she was here tonight to tell you what led up to that. She's got a good memory, you know."

"I know."

"Well, all I remember about it is that I was real hurt. I was hurt deeply because I could see what I'd done to her. I hadn't meant it, and she knew that, and she said that, very dearly. That helped, but not much. It was such an effort for her to say anything critical of anybody at all, especially her own husband. And I hated myself for whatever it was I had done or not done that had driven her to the point where she had to do that. It was as painful for her as for me, I think, and that's what hurt."

"Hard to talk about, huh?"

"You bet. I don't believe I had ever cried in front of anybody since I was about fourteen and learned that my cousin had drowned over in the Rock River. I was the tough guy, you know. But I hated to see a woman cry. Still do. But no one can get to me with tears the way your mom can. Not that she'd ever use crying just to make a point. Never. She's not so quick to cry herself.

"But when she was carefully and lovingly trying to tell me what she needed more of from me—and what she needed less of—well, that made her cry. And it made me cry too. We haven't cried together more than four, five times in forty years, but we cried that afternoon. Hot, Sunday afternoon. We cried when she miscarried between Drew and you. We cried when you left home for good. We cried when we heard about Scott.

And when Tracy made high school homecoming queen, we cried for happiness and pride."

"So did I," Jennifer said. "Dad, I need to know what Mom talked to you about that day. I have to sort out how Jim and I are going to relate to each other. I want to be a good wife. I want to be a biblical wife. I want to be submissive and let him lead in a spiritual sense, but I have to know what that means. Where it starts and ends. What I have to say about anything."

Her father fell silent and studied her before responding. "Times have changed so much," he said. "What was appropriate forty years ago may be the opposite of what you'd want or expect today. While your mom needed me to take more of a leadership role in what I thought were women's things like church and devotions and stuff—you may want to play a bigger role in that yourself."

"But the Bible doesn't change, Dad. Who did I learn that from?"

"I never got the impression you learned it, Jenny, but I confess I hammered you with it constantly."

"I learned it. And you know something? You're still the only person in the world I let call me Jenny."

"Honest?"

"Absolutely. Anybody calls me that but you, I correct them."

"Even Jim?"

"It's never happened, but I would. 'Course he calls me Jenn the way no one else can say it."

"Is the reason you correct everyone because you really don't like the name Jenny and you wish I wouldn't call you that either? You're just afraid to hurt my feelings, right?"

"Wrong. I'll never be anybody else's Jenny, that's all."

"I love you, Jenny."

"Thanks, Dad. I'm glad. Because I have a serious problem, and I need your help."

Nine

As the dessert dishes were removed, Jennifer finished her story—the whole thing, Fred Bishop and all. Her father dragged a linen napkin across his mouth and let it drop to the table before him. He entwined his fingers under his chin and studied his daughter without speaking.

On his face she read deep concern. His brow was knitted, his eyes narrow, his jaw set. As was his manner, he thought a long time before he spoke, and he started with memories that took him back to long before the last few weeks.

"When you were a little girl, I worried about you. I wanted to see a happy face every time I looked at you. You had a smile that would melt ice, but you were independent. You were a thinker. You were a doer. You had justice in your head, and things had to make sense to you.

"You had to have reasons for things. You were never simply happy for no good reason. If you were smiling and bubbly and up, it was because you had seen or heard or done or realized something. If you were happy, I could ask you why, and I would get an answer.

"You felt things deeply, as deeply as an adult by the time you were nine or ten years old. You and your sister were every bit as beautiful as each other. Only she was a people person, eager to make other people happy whether she was happy or not. That made her more popular, more noticed. But I told you the night she was named homecoming queen that you could have won it hands down three years before if it had been your goal. I meant it, and you knew I was right.

"But your priorities were somewhere else. I loved the simplicity of your faith. You questioned the things you didn't understand, and you questioned my explanations for things you didn't think I understood either. And when I admitted I didn't have all the answers, it was no surprise to you, but you were content to trust God and accept by faith that He knew better than we did and that He was trustworthy."

He paused and waited for the smile of recognition that would tell him Jennifer saw the connection between his memories and her encounter with the too-soon grown up Russian boy. "Sergei had to trust you because he had no choice," her father said. "I wish I could see the look on his face when he reads your column tomorrow. Remember it for me, will you, and share it with me someday?"

She nodded, unable to speak.

"Ah, Jenny," he said, picking up his napkin again and twisting it in his hands. "I'm out-of-date. I'm a broken-down old businessman who raised a son and two daughters the best he knew how. I'm tired, but I'm happy, and I'm proud my kids turned out the way they did. Who but Drew could endure the woman he married?"

"Dad!"

"I know. I'm sorry. But she's so obvious it's not even a judgment call. You know I love Francene. Two, three days max, is all I can take at one stretch, but she's a good mother and a good wife. But I was talkin' about Drew. I was trying to make a point about him."

"I know. But Francene thinks the world of you, Dad. It would crush her to know you think she's a nag."

"Did I say that? See, I said nothing about her whiny nagging, and yet you knew what I meant."

Jennifer laughed. "You're terrible."

"You think I'm terrible? Wait till you hear what I think of Tracy's airhead boyfriend."

"Dad!"

"Is that the right use of the term? She uses it herself."

"Not for him, she doesn't," Jennifer said, shocked at her father's uncharacteristic bluntness. "I don't remember the last time I heard you badmouth anyone."

He smiled a knowing smile at her. "Gotcha," he said.

"I don't understand."

"Yes, you do. Or at least you *will* soon enough. I set you up. I stepped out of character. I let you hear how it sounded when I not only talked behind backs, but hit close to home. You'd have been surprised, but a little less shocked, if I had talked about someone else. I could have agreed with you about Fred Bishop. But I don't know the man. I suppose you have the right to complain to me about someone I don't know and whose reputation can't be hurt by your telling the truth about him. But when I start talking about people you know and love, that shocks you. That hurts. How would you have felt if I had said that Fred Bishop sounded like a real louse?"

"I probably wouldn't have given it a second thought, but I still don't know what you're driving at."

He reached across and gripped her wrist gently. "That's all right. You're tired, and have a lot on your mind. What I'm getting at is this: You're not

The Calling

prepared for me to speak the truth even about your brother's tiresome wife or your sister's spacy boyfriend."

He stopped to let it sink in.

"And so," she said, getting the point, "you're not about to speak against my off-the-deep-end fiancé, even if you agree with me."

"Right on the button."

"You're no help."

"In a way I am. You don't hear me defending him, do you?"

"Then you agree with me? He's being unreasonable?"

"No comment."

"Oh, Dad!"

"Not on your life. I'll listen all you want, but my opinion is you're going to marry this guy, and I don't want to go on record saying anything against him."

"So if you can't say something nice about someone, you won't say anything at all. So why should I marry him?"

"Are you wavering?"

Jennifer's eyes filled with tears, so suddenly that even she was shocked. "I'm tired," she said.

"I know," he said, gently stroking the back of her hand. "Maybe you shouldn't think about this tonight."

"That's the problem, Dad. I *have* to think about it constantly. It isn't like I have a choice. And I'm worried about Sergei and Natalya too. What's happened to them and to Jim? Why hasn't he called?"

"Then, while you're spending the last of your energy worrying and wondering, answer my question."

"Am I wavering on whether to marry Jim? Yes!"

Mr. Knight looked at her with compassion. "I'm sorry to hear that," he said. "May I speak in his favor?"

"Of course."

"He's a fine young man. Honest, sincere, spiritual, in love."

"I want him also to be sensitive and caring."

"If he's not, it's temporary."

"How can you know, Dad?"

"It's out of character for him to be insensitive to you, is it not?"

"Well, yes. But how do I get him to snap out of it? Especially when he thinks he is being sensitive. He sees himself as my spiritual guardian, with authority over me."

"And you don't like it."

"No, I don't. But is that just because I'm stubborn and independent? Is that why you brought all that up?"

"That wasn't all I brought up. I also talked about how thrilled I was that you were a thinker and that you thought for yourself. Even if your husband is to have spiritual headship over you, that doesn't mean you leave your brain at the altar. If Jim thinks he can run a marriage and a family and a household without an intelligent, contributing wife, he's going to come to a sad realization."

"Dad, I don't *know* that God hasn't called Jim to be a missionary."

"Of course, you don't. Do you know that God *hasn't* called you?"

"I don't feel a call, but I don't know that you're supposed to feel anything when God calls you."

"Then how does one know? One must feel or sense something. God must impress it upon one's heart some way, Jenny."

"That's just it. Jim thinks God is using *him* to call me. The soon-to-be husband has been called, thus the soon-to-be-wife is along for the ride."

"But you feel fortunate that it happened before you were married because you feel free to decide for yourself."

"I guess."

"And if Jim insists on this and doesn't give it up, the marriage is off unless you feel God tells you otherwise."

She nodded, but didn't speak.

"And what if it had happened a week or a month or a year after you were married? What would be different?"

"That's what I'm afraid of, Dad. Will I magically change overnight when I'm Mrs. James Purcell? Will I not worry whether I feel the calling, as long as Jim is in tune with God?"

George Knight was not in the habit of answering rhetorical questions. He pressed his lips together and displayed both palms to her.

"Dad, this is what has me so torn up. I feel that because this happened now, I was saved by the bell. It's as if I grabbed the last twig before I fell off a cliff. I'm sitting here wearing this diamond, and yet I feel it means nothing. I'm safe, I'm free, I'm not married. If I were married, I'd be trapped, in trouble, no option."

"You'd have an option."

"Divorce is not an option, Dad."

"Of course, it isn't. But you have the same option your mother had. You could sit down with Jim and tell him, as painful as it would be, that there are some things that have to change for the sake of your love, your sanity, your life, your future, your marriage."

"Mom said that to you?"

The Calling

59

He nodded. "Is your marriage worth that, or are you just so relieved to have not tied the knot that you're going to throw it away because of a temporary lapse in Jim?"

"You agree it's *his* problem?"

"Jennifer, I'm not going to get into that. I'm just speaking from your perspective. You think he's wrong in this."

"I think he's wrong for me. I can't speak for him."

"Yet he's trying to speak for you."

"That's it! That's what I can't handle."

"You've prayed about it, thought it through, sought the Lord on it? You don't feel God is calling you to follow Jim in this?"

"I don't."

"And thus you feel that's a sign you shouldn't marry the man?"

"What else can I think? He's not reasonable, even if he is right. The way he presents it makes me want to run the other way, and he's not hearing me, not even listening."

"That sense of commitment and purpose is something you've always admired in him."

"I know, but it's never been directed *against* me before. And that's how I feel, that we're suddenly adversaries."

"You are."

"I know. But am I fighting Jim, or am I fighting God?"

"Do you feel you're fighting God?"

"No, but if I were married, I'd feel I was."

Her father rubbed his ruddy face with both hands, and Jennifer felt bad for keeping him from getting back home. "Jenn, I agree with you that when you're married, you're going to have to work in harmony with Jim, but I really wish you'd see the spiritual headship issue as a last-ditch defense against stalemates. When you're at loggerheads, and you're married, trust God to lead you through Jim. Otherwise, campaign for your opinion. Not for your rights or your position, but for your judgment. You deserve input, and you'll deserve it as much or more then as you do now."

"Dad, my feeling right now is that if I had a heart-to-heart talk with Jim and he was in the same frame of mind he's been in for more than a week, I'd have to tell him that the wedding is off. If God called me to follow Jim or join Jim in missionary work, I believe I'd go. Jim will tell me that God is calling me through him, and I would say I was sorry but I didn't think so, and that would be the end of the relationship. I just know it."

"Then so be it."

"You mean that?"

60   Jennifer Grey Mysteries

"What's the alternative? You give in because you want to marry him, leaving the core of your being at the door, and you give up not just the things you like and want, but the things you feel God has entrusted you with."

"My job, my town, my friends, my church, my responsibilities."

"Right."

"But isn't that what I'm supposed to be willing to give up when I marry?"

"I won't even attempt a guess."

"Dad, I need help, not therapy."

"And I need therapy," he said. He could always make her smile.

"Just tell me you don't think I should get married in my present state of mind."

"I think that's obvious and safe to say."

"So one of us has to change viewpoints."

He cocked his head. "I'd hate to see you make a mistake, Jenn, the way you're thinking. More important, you have to realize this issue could come up again when you're married, and you'll have just as much right and duty to get Jim's attention then as now. Maybe more so. You'll owe it to him."

"Is that it, Dad? Is it a matter of getting his attention?"

"Sure sounds like it."

"Will telling him the wedding is off get his attention?"

"Would that be the only reason you'd say it?"

"No. You know I'd mean it."

"I think you know the answer."

The waiter brought a cordless telephone. "For you, Miss Grey," he said. "And for you," he added, handing the check to her father.

"Jim?" Jennifer said.

"No, Jennifer, this is Leo. Listen, Bram didn't think it was worth bothering you with, but the story is this: Jim and an associate found no one in the room at Rasto's but followed a suspicious car into Indiana, outside the range of their dispatchers. That's why they were unaccounted for until just a little while ago. They finally pulled the car over and discovered three Soviet diplomats who denied having been in the parking lot at Rasto's when the officers arrived. Jim and his partner, guy name of, uh, Carling Eastman—you know him?"

"Sure. Jim's watch commander, a sergeant."

"Yeah, anyway, he and Jim know they followed this car from Rasto's and, of course, suspect these boys are KGB. But now they're in the middle of a hassle, with the diplomats claiming they've been harassed. They're all back in Chicago now and are scheduled for a meeting on Monday in the federal court building with some real mucky-mucks."

"So, where do they think Sergei and Natalya and Bishop are, if not with the three Russians?"

"That's just it. Bishop shows up at a South Side precinct station with a story about the young couple telling him they didn't want his help anymore and making off with the keys to his car. Crazy thing is, he still has his weapon. Why he couldn't overpower a couple of young people is beyond me."

"He was probably sleeping. Sounds phony to me."

"Well, me too, Jennifer, but I don't know what to make of it, and we kind of have to go with his story, whether we imply we believe it or not."

"Believe me, we'll imply that he was irresponsible and sloppy in his technique, at least. Any lead on where the defectors are?"

"Your fiancé thinks he and Eastman were led on a wild goose chase to throw them off the trail. He thinks other Russians, maybe KGB, have already spirited them away. The three diplomats, though, have indicated to somebody at the fed headquarters that they're going to accuse the police of kidnapping the two. Should be interesting."

"What do you want me to do, Leo?"

"Get some sleep. Then enjoy your Sunday. I'll knock out a few update graphs to carry us through the late edition. If you get onto anything late tomorrow, I can take a last minute column by midnight and make the Monday first edition."

"I should hope we'll have something by then. If nothing else, the story of the scheduled diplomatic negotiation."

"I hope we know where the kids are by then," he said.

"I'll be spending time with Jim tomorrow; I'll get what I can."

"He's a little nervous about your date tonight, Jenn. Bram told him you were out with your father, but Jim said he would have known about that."

The waiter hovered as if to suggest that Jennifer was taking too much time on the phone. "Do you need this?" she asked him, covering the mouthpiece.

"When it's convenient, ma'am," he said, meaning, "Yes, as soon as possible."

"I *am* with my father, Leo," she whispered into the phone. "It was a spur-of-the moment thing. Don't worry about it; I'll straighten it out with Jim when he picks me up for church tomorrow."

Ten

"Hoo, boy," George Knight said, settling heavily onto Jennifer's living room couch. "I ate too much. Always do in places that charge like that."

"I did too, Dad, and I'm exhausted. More important, don't let me keep you from getting home before midnight."

"It's already too late for that."

"I mean, I appreciate your coming and spending all this time and—"

"Then let me give you one more reaction, Jenny. Then I'll be outta here so we can both get some shut-eye. You know better'n anybody that I'm no psychologist—but Jim is under a lot of pressure. He's got a lot of changes coming. He's going to change ranks, change life-style, be responsible for two people. My business partner used to tell me not to count on anything of any substance from an employee who's within two months of marriage. They tend to go stir crazy."

"So he's crazy?"

"Only temporarily."

"But what if he doesn't snap out of it?"

"That's your problem," he said, not unkindly.

"How well I know."

Her father stood and reached for his coat. "All I'm saying," he said, "is that you have to attribute some of this, at least, to the fact that he's nervous—maybe without even knowing it—about getting married. He's probably questioning his own ability to take care of you, to lead you the way he knows he should, and he's probably scared to death that you aren't sure he's up to it either."

"But I was sure of it until this."

"Then he may be testing you. He may be forcing you to decide if you really trust him."

"You mean like God with Abraham and Isaac?"

"Yes, except I don't think Jim is doing this on purpose."

"So what should I do?"

"If you agree with that assessment, it gives you an option besides having it out with him or telling him the wedding is off. You can tell him that you're so convinced that he's trustworthy and that he loves you as much as

The Calling

63

he says he does, and that you're so sure he loves God and will continue to seek His will in this, that you'll cast your future with him, trusting him, by God's grace, to do what's best for you as well as for himself."

Jennifer sat down. "That would have sounded so good and so right two weeks ago, but I sure wouldn't be able to say that now, at least not until after a good night's sleep and a lot of prayer."

"But isn't it what you really want to do when you get married, to cast yourself and your future with your husband?"

"Sure, but you have to really feel it, believe it, and mean it."

Jennifer slept long and soundly and was up an hour before Jim was to pick her up for church. While rested, she was nervous. She opened the door as soon as she heard his knock, and for some reason, she sensed it was the old Jim who stood there smiling at her.

She had hoped to start the day off by establishing a bit of cool distance between them. She was going to be cordial and pleasant, but not affectionate or warm. But Jim seemed so much like his old self that she couldn't help responding to his kiss of greeting.

His eyes were alive; he was attentive to her. He seemed to listen and to hear. "I have good news for you," he said. "But it'll have to wait for after church."

During the ride north he reached over the back of the seat to pull the Sunday *Day* from under his Bible.

"I didn't even have time to peek at mine," she said, quickly scanning her column and the sidebar on pages one and two. She liked how it had come out. It was a first edition, so there was no mention of Sergei and Natalya's disappearance.

All during Sunday school and the worship service, Jennifer prayed that her hunch was right that Jim had seen the error of his thinking and that he was at least going to discuss such major decisions with her. Somehow, she hoped, he had snapped out of the emotionalism that had driven him for the past several days.

He was vocal during Sunday school and outgoing after church, greeting people and interacting with them in his usual manner. He beamed when people complimented Jennifer on the exclusive story they had seen that morning.

At lunch she told him she could wait no longer. "What's the news?"

"Well," he said with a twinkle. "All is not as it appears."

"Deep," she teased. "Shall I write it down?"

Jim suddenly grew serious. "There are things I can tell you and things I'm going to tell you even though I shouldn't. Everything has to be off-the-

64 Jennifer Grey Mysteries

record until we've discussed it; then we can decide what you can use and what you can't."

"You mean the good news you were saving for me is not *personal* news?"

"In a way it is. On the whole, no, it's not."

Jennifer was curious because he was obviously sitting on something hot. Yet she held out hope that his seeming reversion to the old personality might mean that things between them would improve too.

"OK," she said simply.

"I have been in contact with Sergei and Natalya."

"Since when?"

"Since early this morning."

"Where are they?"

"We have them in custody. They're safe and hidden. I might be able to take you there, but we have to talk first. Very, very few people know we have them. The Russians are going to be accusing us of having kidnapped them, and if it gets out that we do have them, it would be hard to explain."

"Start over, Jim, please. How did you get in touch with them, and what's their story about leaving Rasto's?"

Jim looked over her shoulder and out the window of the small restaurant. Jennifer felt the chill from the window on her back and pulled her coat collar up to drape it around her shoulders. "This is *really* off-the-record," he said.

"Jim, you're talking to your fiancée, not Dan Rather."

"Jenn, I know. But I have my instructions, and we were the ones who put you onto this story. Now we have to keep control of it."

Jennifer wanted to scream. What he said went against everything she had ever learned or had ever been taught about journalism. Sure, the cops had given her this story. But there could be no strings attached. That's why the later editions of that day's paper would carry hints that regardless of what happened, Fred Bishop was not without implication for some of his incompetencies.

"Meaning?" she said evenly.

"It's just that in exchange for our having given you the scoop, we need assurances that some of the other things you come across may be less appropriate for publication."

Jennifer set her fork down and stared at him. She was sure she reddened. "You sound like some bureaucratic windbag." His eyes narrowed. "I'm sorry, Jim. I hate to talk to you like that, but I hate worse your talking to me like I'm some business associate. Speak English, and remember who you're talking to."

The Calling

Jim appeared shocked. Jennifer knew she was using the frustration that had built up over their personal problems to load her artillery for this battle, but she felt it was worth it. When Jim spoke again, it was obvious she had gotten to him.

"Well, uh, sweetheart, you know I've been told to say that."

"Well, then say so. You only guessed that you were chosen for this assignment with Sergei and Natalya because of me, and now it's very clear that that was the case. So don't pretend to be one of the engineers of it. All of a sudden it's we/they, and it makes me nervous. For one thing, I never agreed to any strings attached to the exclusive interview. Maybe you ought not to tell me where you have the two hidden if the extent of your generosity was one Sunday column."

"That's just it, Jenn. We want you to keep writing about it; I mean *they* want you to keep writing about it. But you can see that some of the information necessarily has to be, ah, colored, or uh, slanted—what am I trying to say, *manipulated* to help us in our negotiations."

Jennifer pushed the uneaten half of her meal away and sat back with her arms folded. Jim looked sheepish, as if he wished he'd remembered not to use "we've" for the police brass when he meant "they."

"Since we're still off-the-record, I have a few questions for *you*," she said, using her most professional and unfriendly tone. "Did you know where the two defectors were when you spotted the Russians in the parking lot at Rasto's and chased them into Indiana?"

"We didn't chase them; we followed them."

"Then why didn't you pull them over where you had jurisdiction, not to mention radio contact?"

"When you're working under the auspices of the United States government, you have jurisdiction anywhere inside the continental United States—Hawaii, Alaska, the District of Columbia, and any U.S. territories."

"You sound like a bureaucrat again, Jim."

"I'm sorry. So do you."

"Are you going to answer my question?"

"I must have missed it."

"Did you know where Sergei Baranov and Natalya Danilin were when you were chasing—excuse me—*following* the Russians through one of the United States' many territories?"

"No."

"How did you know the car you were, ah, following, had KGB agents in it?"

"We didn't. We still don't. They could be diplomats without being KGB."

"And I'm the Easter bunny."

"Sarcasm doesn't become you, Jennifer. It was a rented car. It contained three middle-aged males in dark suits. When we pulled in at Rasto's and ran up to the room, the car pulled away to another location in the lot. That's when we decided to approach it and question the occupants."

"And they said, 'Follow us?' "

"Hardly."

"They pulled away."

"Yes, but not fast."

"So you were following, not chasing."

"OK! At times they appeared to be trying to lose us on the Dan Ryan and the Skyway. So following might have been described as chasing at that point."

"Didn't the fact that they were apparently unaware that Sergei and Natalya were gone lead you to believe they had not abducted them?"

"We didn't know what their involvement might have been. We thought maybe they had taken them, or that some of their associates might have and that they were assigned to see who came to check it out."

"Oh, come on, Jim. I'm not even a cop, and I know that if Russian agents were sent to stake out the site of a kidnapping where a policeman was still there, they're going to be so careful and so secluded that they wouldn't be recognized by the first car that appeared. They had to be staking out the place without knowing that Sergei and Natalya had already left. They were probably hoping to follow the Chicago PD if they tried to move the two somewhere."

"Maybe."

"Did you know where Sergei and Natalya were when you talked to Leo last night?"

"While you were having dinner with your dad—thanks for telling me— no. I didn't know where they were then."

"But you did promise him you would let him, or me, know when you did find them."

"I probably did."

"And does he know?"

"No. but you're about to find out, if you're still with us."

Jennifer shook her head slowly, not taking her eyes off Jim's. "You still don't get it, do you? I'm not with you. I must have independence. I must retain some credibility. Why do you think the paper has the policies it has, and why do you think I have never been allowed to get leads and tips from you before? It's not a you-scratch-my-back-I'll scratch-yours arrangement,

Jim, and I deeply resent it if you or Bram or Eastman or anyone thinks it is."

Jim shrugged. "I don't like to fight with you, Jennifer. I'm not trying to be difficult. The fact is, we know where the two kids are. We're protecting them. We don't want the Russians to know we have them again. You see why?"

"I can guess. I'm just glad to know the disappearance wasn't staged and that the newspaper wasn't used to publicize that for the sake of negotiations."

"It wasn't. And I know now how you're going to feel about this, but what I've been driving at is that we would like to go into tomorrow morning's negotiations under the guise that we have not only not 'kidnapped' Baranov and Danilin, but also that we have reason to believe the Russians have them already. It would scramble their brains and give us the edge in the negotiation."

"I can confidently speak for Max Cooper and Leo Stanton and the *Day*, Jim, you know I can. And I'm telling you, we would not be used for such a purpose, as patriotic as we are and as interested in justice and fair play as we are."

"That's it?"

"That's it."

"You aren't curious to know where they are, how and why they left, and what Bishop's story is?"

"I'm *dying* to know, but if I can't use it, or if I'm asked to publish something else, I won't. Oh, I wish I had never gotten into this mess. If I had known before I went out in the middle of the night, I'd have never gone to Rasto's."

"You know I couldn't tell you over the phone."

"Of course, Jim, but you could have told me before I interviewed them that the police brass was expecting me to play the shill."

"I didn't know that at the time myself," he said. "And I'm not so sure of it now."

"What would you call asking me to slant the story for the sake of the negotiations? Journalism?"

He didn't reply.

"Jim, off-the-record, as a friend, as my fiancée, no obligations, tell me the rest of the story. I will not write it your way, but I won't write it at all either, if you insist."

"I'm still your fiancée? The way you were looking at me, I wondered how long that would last."

68   Jennifer Grey Mysteries

"We need to talk about that, but first, tell me where Sergei and Natalya went, how and why."

"We need to talk about our engagement, but first you want the story? That makes it kind of hard to concentrate, Jenn."

"I know. I'm sorry. I shouldn't have said it that way. Forget that for now."

"But we will talk about it?"

"Of course."

"All right. According to Sergei, Bishop got fresh with Natalya."

"Oh, no."

"Yeah. I guess he didn't really try anything, but he was much more suggestive verbally than he had been even when you were there, and Sergei threatened him. They almost came to blows."

"Bishop admits this?"

"No."

"You know it's true, though, don't you Jim?"

"I believe it's true, yes."

"That's a relief. What's Bishop's story?"

"He says Sergei drugged him by putting something in a drink and that when he woke up several hours later, he discovered they had taken his keys and his car."

"Where was Sergei supposed to get a drug or a drink?"

"Well, *nobody* believes that story, and when we found American whiskey in the room, we knew Bishop had run out for it himself. Sergei's story is that he was so upset with Bishop that Bishop was apologetic and wanted to make it up to him. Sergei said he missed good Russian vodka and that they should share a drink. Of course, Bishop is in big trouble for leaving them, but he admits now that he ran out for some booze and that Sergei, or Natalya, must have put something in it.

"Sergei says that he and Natalya just sipped the booze and pretended not to like it, meanwhile, continuing to fill Bishop's glass until he had drunk several glasses. Then they were just silent and let him talk, and nod, and doze off again. Apparently he collapsed in his chair, and when they took his keys, he didn't even stir. We think Bishop even slept through our phone calls."

"How did Sergei and Natalya think they were going to get away with a policeman's private car, Jim? As soon as he came to, he would have phoned in the information."

"They knew that. That's why they drove north on the Drive for as far as they thought they could, then got onto Sheridan and took it even farther

The Calling 69

up. They dumped the car and used cash to check into a hotel in Highwood."

"That's where they are now?"

He nodded.

"How did you find them?"

"We didn't. We were notified that the car had been located and started a search, but Sergei called a message in to me downtown."

"A message?"

"Yes. It said, 'Tell Miss Grey: Trustworthy.' "

Eleven

"Mean anything to you, Jennifer?"

"Yes!" she said. "But how did *you* know what it meant or who it was from?"

"I didn't until I heard it on the tape. All those calls are taped, so I hurried downtown. When I heard the accent, I knew it was Sergei. By then the call had been traced to Highwood, and we headed back up north."

"I didn't think they could trace a call that fast."

"With the new equipment, calls to the police department are automatically traced, in case the phone goes dead before someone tells his address in an emergency."

"So when you located Sergei, he told you what he meant by trustworthy?"

"Yeah. I was proud of you, Jennifer. I still am."

"Would you be if I kowtowed to your bosses?"

Jim ignored the question. "And Sergei told us his version of how they got away from Fred. Of course, Sergei's in trouble for that."

"And Fred isn't for what he did?"

"Sure. In fact, he'll be suspended for a good long time and maybe reassigned after that. But we don't think it ought to be publicized."

"Making a pass at a young woman defector, leaving her and her fiancé unprotected long enough to buy liquor, drinking on the job, and sleeping on the job?" Jennifer said. "Sounds like a guy who ought to be protected. Coddled maybe."

"C'mon, Jenn. Nobody's going to try to cover for Fred. It's just that you wouldn't have known if I hadn't told you, and—"

"I've been onto Fred from the day we met, Jim! And earlier yesterday he slept through my entire interview with them!"

"—anyway, we want to trade Sergei and Natalya's silence for not pressing charges on what they're guilty of."

"Which is?"

"Grand theft auto."

"Oh, for Pete's sake."

"How can you deny they stole Fred's car?"

The Calling 71

"They didn't intend to steal any car."

"Intent is irrelevant. They took it without permission."

"Put yourself in their places, Jim. Their only hope is their protection in Chicago, and it turns out to be a scoundrel like Fred Bishop. Sergei probably would rather have killed Fred."

"So they're innocent because they could have done worse, Jenn?"

"They're forgivable because they're scared-to-death aliens who don't know where to turn."

"Well, everything I've told you so far is off-the-record, so don't print the stuff about Fred and you won't have to print the stuff about their stealing the car."

Jennifer had to fight a smile.

"What's funny?" Jim asked.

"Their stealing the car is the best part of the story so far," she said.

"Do we have a deal?" he asked.

"I wouldn't call it a deal. I would say you told me a lot of things off-the-record, and unless I get your permission, I can't print them. How is that a deal?"

"You mean what do you get out of it?"

She nodded.

"You get to see them again."

"And I get to write up another interview?"

"Right."

"And what do I say about their disappearance and relocation?"

"Could you see your way clear to imply that it was part of a master police plan to remain elusive?"

Jennifer excused herself for a few minutes. When she came back, she said, "Jim, this morning when you showed up I thought you were yourself again. When I hear you talk like this, you sound like someone else. Is this the way you're going to act when you become a sergeant?"

"A company man you mean?"

"Yeah, I guess that *is* what I mean."

"I don't want to cop out, Jennifer—excuse the pun—but I am only telling you what I've been instructed to tell you."

"Can you see how I feel I'm being used?"

"I guess."

"And do you agree with the logic of your superiors?"

Jim thought a moment. "Let's say I can see your point too. But journalistic standards are not laws. They're rules, and they make a lot of sense, but sometimes it seems it would be better to ignore those standards

72   Jennifer Grey Mysteries

for a higher good. You wouldn't print something that would endanger lives or the security of the country, would you?"

"No, but does that pertain here? What you're talking about is protecting the reputation of a man who should not be protected."

"I admire your convictions, Jennifer, I really do. But even if you convinced me and I totally agreed with you, I can't change what I was asked to communicate. That's the deal. If you want to see Sergei and Natalya for more interviews, we have to keep the stuff about Fred Bishop off-the-record."

"Is that Sergei and Natalya's wish too?"

"They're willing to abide by it so they don't suffer for stealing the car."

"You'd actually press charges on that?"

"Bishop might."

"But only if they pressed charges against him for his failure, right?"

"Probably."

"What if they tell me the Bishop story *and* why they took the car, but still don't press to get him in trouble?"

"Still no good. No deal. You can't use it."

"Then I don't want to interview them again."

"You're not curious about where they are and how they are?"

"Of course, but I'm being used, and there are too many strings."

"Will you be printing that fact?"

"That the police department is trying to manipulate the story?"

"Yes."

"No. I won't. I'll give you that much."

"Thanks."

Jennifer didn't respond.

The tension between them was thick as Jim drove in silence to the home where they had chosen to begin their married lives. It was barren, and the heat had been turned way down. Jennifer wondered why he had brought her there.

Jim pointed to a short step ladder in the living room, then brought a wood crate from the kitchen. They sat awkwardly facing each other. Jennifer was still upset over the lunch argument and had decided not to speak unless Jim spoke first.

"Can we disagree and still love each other?" he asked suddenly.

"About journalism and public relations, of course," she said. "I can't expect a nonjournalist to be sympathetic with journalistic standards."

"And I can't expect a noncop to understand how important it is to us to protect our reputation and our people."

"Fred Bishop is one of your people, Jim? Do you put yourself in his—"

The Calling

"Jenn, we've been over that. Can we leave that subject?"

"Yes, I'm sorry. But if I thought you saw yourself as some sort of a brother to Fred Bishop, I'd hate it."

"You know better than that."

She did, but she decided not to say so.

"I suppose you're wondering why I've called this meeting," he joked. She forced a smile. "I just thought this was as good a place as any to discuss our future."

Jennifer knew she looked distant, but she didn't care. He continued. "I feel God has used this encounter with the Russians to confirm my calling to missionary work. I need and want your support."

Still she didn't respond.

"Do I have it?" he asked.

Jennifer felt herself becoming emotional, but she fought back the tears. "How could I not support you if God has called you?" she asked.

"I sense you're not totally behind me, though, Jenn."

"I'm not."

"Why?"

"Because it carries too many implications. If I'm going to be your wife, I must share the call."

"I feel that way, yes."

"Jim, I don't feel the call, and please don't tell me that my call is coming through you. I have obligations."

"But weren't you going to sacrifice some of your obligations to get married, just like I would?"

"You never asked me to give up my work. I'm under contract. You know the *Day* has made a substantial financial commitment to me and my column."

"I know you're almost in six figures, but I can't believe you wouldn't give that up for your faith."

"Jim! How can you say that? I'm thrilled and overwhelmed by how much the *Day* thinks I'm worth, but I can live without the money."

"Then why did you mention the financial commitment?"

"Because they've signed me to a long-term contract. It runs almost four more years. They've advertised my column, built their front page around it, won awards because of it. And Jim, you *know* God has used it. They have never restricted one thing I've wanted to write, and they've syndicated the column all over the country. I can reach more people in one day than I could reach in a year of public speaking."

"But if God called you away from that to a ministry that wasn't in the limelight—?"

74 Jennifer Grey Mysteries

"I'd go in a minute. But He hasn't yet."

"Have you examined whether you just don't want God to call you out of such a public role?"

"Yes! I believe I'm open to Him, Jim. I really do. But your questions make me wonder if you're jealous of my visibility."

Jim stood and shook his head. "No," he said. "I've searched myself for that. Really, Jennifer. In fact, if anything, I take too much pride in your accomplishments and notoriety."

"Then give me the benefit of the doubt. I can believe you're not jealous; if you can believe I'm not hanging onto the job for my ego or my budget."

He walked to the drapeless window and stared out into the snow. "I've been thinking about this house," he said. "And maybe you're right. Maybe we should go ahead and buy it, and I can leave the police department and study at one of the local Christian colleges or seminaries."

Jennifer stood and moved to stand behind Jim, but she didn't touch him. "So I can keep working and support us?" she suggested.

He turned to face her. "Is that too much to ask?"

"Not at all," she said. "It will give me time to get used to the idea of missionary work. And it will allow me to fulfill my commitment to the *Day*."

"But what if you don't feel the call when the time comes to go?"

"I'll decide what I'm going to do before I marry you, Jim. Once we're married, I go where you go. But I still want to be involved in the decisions that affect us. I won't question how God calls a person, but I confess I wonder about the quickness of your decision. I don't like what it has done to you."

"What has it done to me? I've felt like I was walking on air ever since."

"You have been. You've been unreachable. I haven't felt like I could communicate with you until today, and then we were arguing about something else."

"I'm sorry about that."

"Don't be. In a way, I loved it. We were disagreeing, but we were communicating. I went several days without feeling we were making any real contact at all."

Jim put his hands on her shoulders and rested his forehead on hers. "That's scary," he said.

"Yes, it certainly is," she said. "I was prepared to give you your ring back today and call the wedding off."

He winced and closed his eyes. "And now?"

"I love you. I know that. But I cannot be shut out of your life or just dragged along for the ride."

The Calling

"Do you think I should go to school and prepare for missionary work?"

Jennifer didn't respond quickly. When she did, she said, "Jim, I just can't argue with you about God's call on your life. If He called you, He called you. Who am I to say that He didn't, or wouldn't? God's ways are not our ways, though He does honor us when we honor our commitments.

"God's calling you from a successful law enforcement career may just be the test you think it is. But you're a good policeman, highly thought of, about to be promoted. That carries with it a certain implied commitment too, doesn't it? Your employers are counting on you in their future. I think God wants you to consider that carefully."

Jim took the crate back to the kitchen and walked Jennifer out to the car. As they headed to her apartment, he said, "For strictly personal reasons, I wish you'd come with me to see Sergei and Natalya."

"I can't, Jim. I am so fond of them that I'm afraid if I meet with them again, I'll be tempted to give in on my convictions and write the story your people want, rather than the one that should be told."

"But, Jennifer, I got a chance to really talk to them this morning."

"What do you mean?"

"Well, they asked about us. About why we were different. They've met several officials since they arrived, some they liked and some they didn't. But Sergei said he sensed something different about you and me, mostly you, I'm sorry to admit."

"So you got a chance to tell them about our faith?"

"Yes. For almost an hour."

"Almost an hour? I had no idea you had that much time with them."

"Yeah. He called downtown very early. Apparently, that hotel gets the morning paper just after midnight. I'm not sure when he got it, but as soon as he read it, he called in his message. They'd like to see you, Jennifer. And I think you might be able to add to what I said this morning."

"No wonder you seemed so high when you picked me up today. Maybe you are cut out for missionary work."

"You'll come see them then?"

"Not just yet."

Twelve

Leo reacted even more strongly than Jennifer had when she told him what the police wanted from her. Through the phone she could hear him slam a fist on his desk. "Come on in, Jennifer. I want to talk about this in person."

When she arrived, he was still fuming. "Imagine the nerve of those guys! I don't know how long I've been in this business, and we still can't seem to get through to city officials that we aren't a PR sheet."

"So I made the right decision?" Jennifer asked.

"Of course. I just hope they don't go after someone from the *Trib* or *Times* now."

"Oh, I never thought of that. How can we ensure against it?"

"We can't, unless you want to be guilty of the same things the cops are guilty of. Tell them that we're gonna run with everything you heard this morning unless they keep it away from our competitors. Wouldn't that be a wonderful way to show our consistency?"

"And trustworthiness."

"Yeah. All I'm sayin' is that we have weapons we could use too. We just choose not to because we play by the same rules we expect others to play by."

They sat staring at the floor, enjoying each other's company and their common misery. Jennifer felt good to be with her boss, who understood and agreed at least on this.

"What I want you to do," Leo said, "is keyboard everything you know at this point, as if you were going to use it."

"You mean write it up in column form?"

"If that would help. I just want to be sure we have everything at this point, whether we are free to use it or not."

"You think something will break and we *will* be able to use it?"

"You never know. It's good to be prepared."

When Jennifer finished several hours later, she had composed four columns. "There's a lot in each one that cannot be used," she told Leo. "It's a pity."

76

The Calling

"It sure is," he said, calling them up on his video screen and scanning them quickly. "They're beautiful. I feel like calling the Chicago PD or the feds or whoever and threatening to use them."

"Too bad that's not how we work, Leo."

"I'm glad it's not. At least we have the information for posterity. Any ideas for tomorrow's column?"

"I'm not supposed to have a column in Monday's paper."

"I know, but we're gonna look silly if we don't follow up on the hottest story of the year."

"The year isn't very old, Leo."

"You never were any good at taking compliments. You know what I mean. We can't be silent on this one. We'll look terrible."

"You want me to write a follow-up story with everything I have that's *not* off-the record?"

"How much is that?"

"Precious little."

"You used a lot the first time, and what's left, other than what you learned today, would be fluff, right?"

"Right."

"I'd almost rather be silent than not bring the reader up-to-date."

"Me too, Leo."

He sat teething on his unlit cigar and staring past Jennifer. "Jenn," he said quietly, as if something had just come to him, "I wonder what the federal authorities think about this. I wonder if they even know about it."

"They must know most of it," she said, "because they entrusted Baranov and Danilin to the Chicago PD, and I'm guessing they've kept in close touch."

"I'm gonna call them."

Leo dialed and let it ring for a long time. "Somebody's gotta be there even on a Sunday," he told Jennifer. "Maybe no receptionist, but surely someone working on this case and preparing for tomorrow's—

"Oh, hello, yeah, who've I got? . . . Ah, Leo Stanton from the *Day*. Just wondering if Chick Alm is around today? . . . Yeah, I'll wait." Leo motioned to Jennifer to listen in on the other phone.

"Hey, Leo," Agent Alm said, "It's been a long time. What's shakin?"

"Oh, I'm just looking for some more background information on this Russian defector thing."

"Yeah, you and every other paper in town. I just got off the phone with the *Tribune*, and the *Sun-Times* called earlier."

"They base their questions on our piece, Chick?"

"A little. But mostly on what they got from this Bishop."

"The cop?"

"Yeah! They're askin' if we're gonna deport these kids for rollin' him and stealing his car. He told 'em if he hadn't fallen on his weapon when he was hit, they'd have taken that too."

"What *are* you going to do, Chick?"

"We don't know yet, Leo. We were really hoping nothing like this would go down before the meeting with the Soviets tomorrow. They'll probably make out like Baranov and Danilin are criminals in the Soviet Union and that they want 'em back so they can prosecute. That's gonna make your story in today's paper look sick."

"Chick, I have to ask you. Were you aware of this before Bishop told you?"

"Ah, funny you should ask. We off-the-record?"

"I'd rather not be, but if we have to be."

"Off-the-record, no. The cops told us there was a mix-up. The officer who was supposed to take over for Bishop was late or went to the wrong place or something, and they got their signals crossed. Then they decided to move the couple. That was all we knew. But you know, the guy from the *Times* told me this morning that one of the cops on this case is the boyfriend or husband or something of your columnist, the one who wrote the story. He says she got a break, so he wants one. I couldn't give him anything, and you can't print what I said either, Leo. We're keeping it under wraps until this meeting tomorrow."

"Chick, when the other two papers print this stuff about the Russians overpowering Fred Bishop, your cover is blown. The Russians will know you have Baranov and Danilin in custody again. Chick, I think you've been lied to by the Chicago PD, and I know the other papers have been lied to by Bishop. The police can't be too thrilled when all that comes out, because it's going to make it difficult for them to reprimand Bishop when he comes off looking like a victim."

There was silence on the other end for several seconds. Then, "I see what you mean, Leo. I'll talk to our police contacts and get back to you. But do me a favor and don't print any of this."

"I've got until late tonight," Leo said. "And it won't break my heart if the competition comes out with the wrong story. But we have to print something, Chick. If I don't hear from you, I'm going to assume the restrictions are off and we can go with everything we've got. Fair enough?"

"I'm sorry, Leo, I can't let you do that."

"Why not?"

The Calling 79

"Because I might get tied up and be unable to get back to you. Then what? You print something that may be true but damaging to our diplomacy and we've all got trouble. Promise me you'll wait until you hear from me."

Leo hung up. "Why'd you do that, Leo?" Jennifer said. "He's going to think you're going to press without his permission."

"That guarantees he'll call me. You'd better get to Bram and get the same kind of guarantee."

"Norman, I must see you," Jennifer said when she reached Bram at his home.

"Jennifer, do yourself a favor and interview the kids on *our* terms, huh?"

"I can't do that, Norm, and you know it."

"You don't appreciate the tip that got you the big exclusive this morning?"

"I *do*, but I didn't know it had a price. It made you guys look pretty good for being so wonderful to Chicago's guests, but I could have included Bishop's first bit of inappropriate talk to both Natalya Danilin and to me, and I could have included the fact that he slept a couple of hours while I was interviewing Natalya and Sergei. That wasn't off-the-record. I could still use it."

"Let *us* handle the discipline, Jennifer. What he did later was worse, we admit, and he's going to suffer for it."

"*You're* going to suffer for it."

"How do you mean?"

"He's gone to the other papers, and they've gone to the feds, with an invented story. It looks bad for the defectors and should gain a lot of sympathy for Bishop. How are you going to suspend him or reassign him or whatever it is you have planned if the public thinks the poor man was mugged by Russian criminals?"

"Let's get together, Jennifer. I'm supposed to meet Federal Agent Chick Alm at my office in an hour, and this must be what he wants to discuss. Can you be there before that? I'd like to have all the ammo I can."

Not long later, after Jennifer had laid out everything she knew from the first call from Jim at two in the morning until now, Bram asked Alm if Jennifer could sit in on their meeting. "Only if she can shed some light on the problem, Norm. I'm telling you, we're going to have to have it out about why our office didn't get the straight dope on what happened."

"Believe me, she can help," Bram said. "You can trust her."

80   Jennifer Grey Mysteries

Bram had to take a lot of heat from Alm about not only the lack of communication between the federal and the local agencies, but also the misinformation that was apparently fostered. After they heard Jennifer's rundown of what had happened, they sat staring at each other.

Finally, Alm spoke. "Norm, we've got to let the *Day* print the whole story. And you've got to can Fred Bishop."

"He's as good as gone," Bram said. "And there's another wrinkle, Chick. You remember you told me the Soviets wanted Baranov and Danilin at the discussion tomorrow, no strings attached? Well, Sergei and Natalya have a condition."

"I can't wait to hear it," Alm said.

"They'll come if they can be accompanied at all times by Jennifer Grey."

With the freedom to print anything and everything she thought was relevant, including the bungling of information between the police and federal agents, Jennifer had to fight to watch the speed limit as she wheeled north.

Two uniformed police officers outside the hotel room door made it obvious that security was tight. They had apparently been tipped that Jennifer was coming and was welcome, because one opened the door and the other waved her in.

Sergei and Natalya were huddled in a corner with Jim, but three other plainclothesmen were also in the room, one on the phone and two chatting by the window. Natalya squealed and jumped to her feet when she saw Jennifer. They embraced, and so, this time, did Jennifer and Sergei. And of course, Jim and Jennifer. "Somebody win a gold medal?" one of the cops quipped.

"Is there another room where we can talk?" Jennifer asked Jim. He led her to a smaller suite where she briefed him on what had happened.

"I'm happy for you," he said. "So you were right all along. And I was wrong."

"You were doing what you were told," she said.

"That's no excuse. I've got a lot to learn."

"So do I, sweetheart," she said.

They returned to Sergei and Natalya, and the couples sat directly across from each other in love seats. "Thanks for inviting me to the meeting tomorrow," Jennifer said.

"It wasn't exactly an invitation," Sergei said. "It was a condition."

"I know, but I'm grateful. It means a lot to me."

"Your article was wonderful," Natalya said.

The Calling 81

"Thank you."

"Really," Sergei said. "I know my message got us caught again. But I wanted to tell you that you had for sure proved that you were trustworthy. If I had read the article before it was printed, I would have changed not a word."

"He means it," Natalya said. "I know because he has been saying that all day."

Jennifer filled them in on all that had happened from her perspective since the last time she saw them. They were shocked to hear of Bishop's account of their crisis.

"I want to interview you for several columns this week, but most of them are written already. They just have to be updated with quotes from you, and I need to add the information about Officer Bishop going to the other papers with his story."

"Will the other papers tell it the way he told it?" Sergei asked.

"In a way, I hope so," Jennifer said. "I know that sounds a little cruel, but if they print that without substantiating it, it's their own fault. We would certainly never run a story like that without making sure of it first."

"But your article will make them look bad, won't it?" Natalya asked. "Or do people here like to believe lies over the truth?"

"When lies are all they read, it's all they can believe," Jennifer said. "But when both the truth and a lie are printed, the truth looks and reads and sounds like truth. People will know the difference. Especially when Officer Bishop is fired. They wouldn't fire him if they thought he was telling the truth, would they?"

Sergei and Natalya shook their heads. "We want to tell you whatever else you need to know, because we know we can trust you," Sergei said. "But there is one thing that worries us. These men who call themselves Soviet diplomats, they are KGB for sure. You must promise that you will not let us out of your presence tomorrow. They will want to meet with us privately for a few minutes, I am sure of it. And no one can imagine how much they can accomplish in those few minutes. I heard of a Russian defector to England who was taken into a back room for less than five minutes, and when the 'diplomats' returned, they had taken a self-developing photograph of him and attached it to a phony arrest record from Russia. They also had a written confession signed by him, along with his request not to be interviewed by the British again. Do we have your word that you will stay with us all the time?"

"Every second," Jennifer said.

Thirteen

Late Sunday evening, when Jennifer had finished getting the information she needed for her columns and started feeling the pressure to get downtown to the office, a message came for her.

"Ma'am," one of the policemen said, "we've been asked to tell you to call your boss."

"Shall I wait down here, Jennifer?" Leo wanted to know.

"Nah, I don't think so. It's going to be dynamite stuff."

"So Chick Alm told me. I'm proud of you. You're gonna let me read about it in the morning, huh?"

"It's basically the stuff you saw earlier today anyway, Leo. They've just corroborated everything and clarified a few things. It'll be better, but not wholly different."

"And are we scooping the competition?"

"As far as I know."

"All right, I have arranged it so you can just key your copy directly in to composition, as long as they have it by midnight. Watch your length and your formatting, and I'll give you a call after I've read the paper at home in the morning."

"Leo, do me a favor, huh?"

"Anything."

"Call me closer to noon."

"You've got it."

Jennifer intended to get brief good-byes out of the way and get downtown in plenty of time, but it was apparent that something was on Sergei's mind.

His serious look accompanied myriad questions designed to keep her there. "Well, I better run," she said.

"Ah, one more thing," he said, looking around and leaning in closer to Jennifer, Natalya, and Jim. "I have many questions regarding what Jim talked to us about today."

Jennifer couldn't help looking at her watch. She hated herself for not hiding it better, but it was nine o'clock. Sergei hesitated. "You have no more time?"

82

The Calling 83

She decided that if she left by nine-thirty, she would be OK since she wasn't creating a column from scratch. "It's all right," she said, also leaning toward him.

"This was something new to us," Sergei said. "We are aware of Christians in the Soviet Union, but we have never known what they *really* believe. Schools in Russia are not afraid to teach what religions believe, because they are so convinced that they are all stupid and baseless, and they ridicule them."

"So you did learn something of religion there?"

"Oh, yes. But, of course, we also had courses in dialectical materialism and atheism."

"Actual courses?"

"Oh, yes."

Natalya explained, "Neither Sergei nor I am still an atheist, though we were when we were children. It's sort of a special thing with teenagers in Russia to secretly believe in God or to at least allow for the possibility that there is a God."

"It's a form of rebellion," Sergei said. "I suppose young people in this country go against what they are taught just to get a reaction."

Jim and Jennifer nodded. Natalya continued. "We learned that Christianity was a set of beliefs like all other religions. Hindus have their beliefs, Moslems theirs, Buddhists theirs, and Christians theirs. Christianity was begun in the first century when Jesus was born, and a group of radical Jews believed He was the Son of God. When He was put to death, they made some sort of a martyr of Him, and they believed He came back to life and went to heaven, and that He's coming back someday."

"That's pretty good," Jennifer said.

"Yes, but we thought Christians in Russia—the Russian Orthodox and the Baptists were sects, like other religions. We thought they studied their Bibles and said prayers and did good works, like everyone else."

"They probably do," Jennifer said.

"But if they know this faith the way Jim told us today," Sergei said, "it is much more than that, is it not?"

"I think so," Jennifer said. "What do you think about it?"

Neither spoke for a moment. "We aren't sure what to think," Sergei said finally. "I find it intriguing and different, just because it is so personal, but the personal quality of it repels me as well."

"Why?"

84   Jennifer Grey Mysteries

"Because it is so far removed from anything we've ever heard that we wonder if we can adjust our thinking to allow for this approach. Is it fairly common in America?"

"What aspect are you referring to, Sergei?"

"This, this *personal* approach. Jim talked about knowing God, knowing Jesus Christ. And there is the exclusivity."

"The exclusivity?" Jennifer asked.

"Yes, where Jesus is supposed to have said that He was the only way to God. We have been taught that all religions believe that they are the way to God, but that only some small cults are the ones who believe they are the only true religion. Now you say this is true of Christianity and the Man who founded it. Yet Christianity is no small group or sect. It is a major world religion, and the dominant religion in America. Do most Americans feel that their religion is the only way to God?"

Jim caught Jennifer's eye, then spoke. There are many who believe as we do that the Bible is God's Word and that where it quotes Jesus as saying He is the only way to God, it is a true account of what He said. We don't understand it all, but we believe it. You know what I mean?"

"I think so. Would you know if the Russian Orthodox and the Baptists also believe that each individual Christian can know God and commune with Christ?"

"I'm afraid I don't know," Jim said. "But I'm sure that many Christians in Russia enjoy that relationship with God."

"That is shocking," Natalya said.

"Why shocking?" Jennifer asked.

Natalya appeared unable to express herself. Sergei offered, "It is just so different from what we have heard or known." Natalya nodded.

"Does it appeal to you?" Jennifer asked.

Sergei shook his head. Natalya said, "No. It is too different—puzzling. And we wonder why it is not known better. It would seem that this would in many ways be a more attractive religion than the sets of beliefs and creeds."

"Oh, we find it so," Jennifer said.

"It makes you different," Sergei said.

"It's supposed to," Jennifer said. "It doesn't always, because we often get in the way of God working in our lives. But we are supposed to be known by how we love one another and other people."

"I think that is what we see," Natalya said.

Jennifer asked, "Why does it not appeal to you then, if you think it would be more attractive than other religions you've heard about?"

The Calling

85

"Well," Sergei began, "it seems it would be more attractive to religious people. I can see why you would like this religion better than another, but we are not religious people. We allow for the possibility that God exists, but it is such a jarring thing to think that He wants to be friends with people."

Sergei paused, then added, "It's very interesting. A new lesson for us. We like to study and learn."

"Can you think about the fact that God might love you and care about you personally?" Jennifer asked. "I mean, if He made you, would He not want to communicate with you?"

Sergei smiled at her. "Like your husband-to-be, you are going to be a proselyter, no?"

"I don't know," she said. "Maybe."

"Jim tells me that he may go to other countries to tell people about his religion."

Jennifer looked at Jim and smiled.

"Tell me," Sergei said, "how many people in the United States believe as you do?"

"Many," Jim said.

"How many?"

"Hundreds of thousands, maybe more."

"How many do not?"

"Many, many more," Jim admitted.

"You are a persuasive speaker," Sergei said. "Do you tell those who do not agree with you or those who do not know?"

"Do I tell them?"

"About what you believe. I should think that people in America who are not atheists, even those who are, you would want to tell them about this. If you will be going to other countries to tell it, you must tell it here too."

"I do."

"Ah," Sergei said, nodding. "And there are no more to tell here?"

"Well, it's not that. I don't really tell it as much as I should."

"Why are you going far away to do this then?"

"I feel it's what God wants me to do."

Sergei smiled and looked at Natalya. "I would think you should tell everybody here before you go somewhere else."

"Perhaps," Jim said.

"You meet many people in trouble here," Sergei said. "Why would you want to go somewhere else?"

"I don't know," Jim said. "Maybe I should just tell everyone, wherever I am."

86   Jennifer Grey Mysteries

"Maybe," Sergei said. "I don't know. I am not a believer and maybe never can be. But your beliefs make you different, and you are in many ways as devout as a communist."

Jennifer wondered if this young man with the thick accent had hit on something and expressed it better than she had been able to in a week's worth of trying.

The next morning Jennifer's column hit the city, and Fred Bishop, like a bomb. It exploded in the faces of the competition who had published pieces critical of the agencies involved and sympathetic to Fred Bishop. As predicted, the truth rang true, and a general outcry went up.

When Jennifer showed up at the federal building, Sergei and Natalya had already had an encounter with the diplomats in the lobby. They requested a brief meeting with just them, insisting that they had urgent messages for the pair from their families. Natalya's eyes filled with tears, but Sergei quickly turned her aside and whispered in her ear. Jim and his associates expressed Sergei and Natalya's request against the brief meeting, but when it appeared to Sergei that the Americans were wavering, he began struggling and shouting, "This is not part of the agreement! Miss Grey is not here!"

The Americans hustled Sergei and Natalya away, and now the Russians waited in a meeting room while Jennifer and Jim and several federal agents waited with the young defectors in a sitting room.

Jim whispered to Jennifer. "Sergei really got to me last night."

"Really?"

"Yeah. I don't doubt God was speaking to me at the missions conference last week, but I'm wondering if I didn't overreact to my failures in sharing my faith by thinking that I had to become a full-time missionary."

In a way Jennifer was happy to hear him say that, but she wished she had the courage to tell him that he should let her know when he decided for sure. She thought it might have an impact on when they should get married. If he was that undecided and easily swayed, she wondered if he was ready for the big step. And she was afraid she wasn't.

But she remembered her father's counsel and knew that some of Jim's uncharacteristic immaturity was due to the impending marriage. She was confident God would give her the assurance that the wedding was the right step sometime during the next few weeks before the big day.

If He didn't, she would have to tell Jim that it would be postponed. The thought of it made her smile. No way was that going to happen.

A federal marshal stepped into the room. "Mr. Baranov, Miss Danilin, Mrs. Grey?" They rose and approached him. "Follow me, please."

The Calling 87

Sergei and Natalya were apprehensive, nervous. They expected to face the Russian diplomats when they entered the big meeting room, as did Jennifer.

But no one was there. Jennifer and the kids sat next to each other on one side of a huge mahogany table and watched the marshal leave, assuming he would escort the three Russians back into the room. Sergei whispered something to Natalya. He turned to Jennifer, still whispering. "Don't be surprised at anything. They will try everything to get us alone. If you are called out for a message, do not go, or I will go with you."

Jennifer smiled and patted his arm to assure him she would not leave them. "I wrote all that in my column today," she whispered, "your predictions of what they might try. They will look silly if they try any of that."

The marshal came back. "Mr. Baranov, Miss Danilin, you are free to go," he said, smiling.

"Wait!" Sergei shouted, standing. "It's a trick!"

"It's no trick," the marshal said. "I saw them leave myself. They drove away." He pulled a piece of paper from his pocket. "Their message is this: 'The Union of Soviet Socialist Republics has no more interest in Baranov and Danilin, betrayers of the motherland. We are satisfied they have not been detained against their will, and they are refused reentry in the USSR.'"

Sergei was still squinting in disbelief. "I do not understand," he said.

"I might have had something to do with it," the marshal said, leaning over the table, both hands resting in front of Sergei. "Sit down, please, Mr. Baranov." When Sergei was seated, the marshal told him what had happened.

"I searched their briefcases before they entered this room," he said. "Standard procedure. They're used to it. Interesting thing was, one of them had a Polaroid camera. And I had just read your column, Mrs. Grey. The one about the fact that they might try to take Sergei and Natalya into another room and photograph them.

"I asked them if they had seen the morning paper, and they said, 'Only the *Times*.' I felt it was only fair that they see the *Day*. Wouldn't you agree?"

Jennifer nodded, smiling. Sergei embraced Natalya.

"Next thing I knew," the marshal said, "they were handwriting a message. Then they were gone. Welcome to America, kids. You're free!"

Dear Reader:

Please let us know how you feel about Barbour Books' Christian Fiction.

1. What most influenced you to purchase Jennifer Grey Mystery Collection #1, #2, #3 (Please circle one)?

   _____ Author   _____ Recommendations

   _____ Subject matter   _____ Price

   _____ Cover / titles

2. Would you buy other books in the Jennifer Grey Mystery series by this author?

   _____ Yes   _____ No

3. Where did you purchase this book?

   _____ Christian book store   _____ Other

   _____ General book store   _____ Mail order

4. What is your overall rating of this Collection?

   _____ Excellent _____ Very good _____ Good _____ Fair _____ Poor

5. How many hours a week do you spend reading books? _____ hrs.

6. Are you a member of a church? _____ Yes _____ No

   If yes, what denomination?_____

7. Please check age

   _____ Under 18   _____ 25-34   _____ 45-54

   _____ 18-24   _____ 35-44   _____ 55 and over

Mail to: **Fiction Editor**
Barbour Books
P.O. Box 1219
Westwood, NJ 07675

NAME _____

ADDRESS _____

CITY _____ STATE _____ ZIP _____

Thank you for helping us provide the best in Christian fiction!

Jennifer didn't think she'd be writing her syndicated column on her wedding day. But she didn't expect to be kidnapped either! Four hostile terrorists want national attention for their cause and through Jennifer's column, plan to get it. The question is, Did Jennifer put enough clues into the column she is forced to write at gunpoint?

Jerry B. Jenkins, is the author of more than ninety books, including the popular Margo Mystery Series, co-author of the best-selling *Out Of The Blue* with Orel Hershiser, and *Hedges*. Jenkins lives with his wife, Dianna, and three sons at Three-Son Acres, Zion, Illinois.

Jerry B. Jenkins

VEILED THREAT

Book Six In The Jennifer Grey Mystery Series

Flip over for another great
Jennifer Grey Mystery!
THE CALLING

BARBOUR BOOKS
Westwood, New Jersey

Copyright © MCMXCI   Barbour and Company, Inc.
P.O. Box 1219
Westwood, New Jersey 07675

All Rights Reserved
Printed in the United States of America
ISBN 1-55748-168-7
91   92   93   94   95   5   4   3   2   1

VEILED THREAT

One

Jennifer Grey didn't expect to be writing her nationally syndicated *Chicago Day* front page column on her wedding day. Nor for three weeks after that in Hawaii where she and Jim Purcell expected to start their married life.

But then she didn't expect to still be single at the end of her wedding day either.

Things had gone smoothly once she and Jim had finally set a date—Sunday, August 19, 3:00 P.M. Jennifer had had to carefully explain to her mother, Lillian Knight, why the wedding really had to be in Chicago rather than Rockford. Her father, George, had been understanding and was an ally in the brief skirmish.

"All of our friends are here, Mom," Jennifer explained. "Jim's attendants are all from the church or the police department, and mine are from the church or the paper. Anyway, I promised only a few people from the national media that they could come, and Rockford is just not an easy place to get to."

Jennifer had heeded the advice of her boss, Leo Stanton, to resist the temptation to write about her wedding before it happened. "We'll just run your picture with a note that you're on your honeymoon," he said. "Then you won't get all the crazies and the groupies."

About four hundred friends and relatives had indicated that they would attend. Jennifer wished the church was air-conditioned. The forecast was for clear skies and ninety-nine degrees with humidity not far below that. When she awoke from a fitful sleep, partly due to the jitters and partly to the heat and humidity which invaded with the dawn, she knew the forecast had been too timid. By church-time, it was eighty degrees, and the wind was dead.

By noon it would be one hundred, and under a cloudless sky, no relief was in sight. Jennifer was glad she had insisted her parents stay in a hotel in Chicago the night before the wedding. "That way you'll be fresh, cool, and have a place to change without a long drive to look forward to." And The Consulate was a classy place. She picked it out herself.

3

4 Jennifer Grey Mysteries

Just before Jennifer left her apartment for church that morning, she got a call from Candy Atkins, her matron of honor. "Game plan still intact?" Candy asked.

Jennifer assured her it was. "I just wish Jim's parents were alive to share this day with him," she added.

Jennifer was taking her wedding dress and luggage, everything, to church with her. After church, someone would run out and grab something for the women to eat so they could spend the early part of the afternoon getting ready and supervising the florist.

At church Jennifer got tired of answering whether she was "ready for the big day today" and also of explaining that Jim had decided to attend another church that morning.

He was still hung up on some of the old traditions—like the groom not seeing the bride before the ceremony on the day of the wedding, but this was the first time for him. Jennifer had been widowed after only a short marriage to Scott Grey. She didn't want to think about Scott so much that morning during church, but she knew it was inevitable. The old emotions came storming back—the deep love she had felt for him, the excitement of their courtship, the wedding, the gifts, the friends, the honeymoon, the new home, the new church, the new social circle.

And the stark, black day in the winter when her phone rang and a state trooper asked kindly if he could come and visit her briefly. The premonition. She knew. She took the news of the accident almost in stride, yet found herself still grieving months later, almost as if in a trance.

Her new job at the *Day* helped, but it was being moved to the police beat and meeting the young, tall, blond policeman Jim Purcell that really healed her hurts, her memories. Theirs had been a difficult courtship, with Jennifer not knowing her true feelings toward him until he was in trouble, suspected of being a dope-dealing dirty cop with all the cards stacked against him.

After he was cleared and they found themselves deeply in love, moving headlong toward marriage, Jim suddenly felt the call to foreign missions. It was almost the end of them. Not that Jennifer wasn't just as devout a Christian. But she had discovered a side of Jim she had not suspected. An impetuous, emotionally oriented, impulsive side that scared her.

But they had survived that too. Jim realized that his conviction, the work of God in his life related to telling others about his faith, began with the people around him. He didn't have to travel halfway around the world to be a missionary, and if he wasn't really to begin with his own circle of friends and acquaintances, he would never succeed anywhere else either, no matter how far away.

Veiled Threat

He had begun a Bible study at work for other Christian policemen and several who were not. Three had become Christians over the past six months. Just as important, Jim was growing.

When Jennifer found her mind had shifted from Scott to Jim, she was grateful, but even that thought brought her back to Scott. She knew she would have to deal with that somehow. Jim had been so understanding when she had wanted to talk about her late husband. And while he hadn't said so, she knew that after the wedding, Jim would probably be much more comfortable if she just dropped the subject. Jim was to be the primary focus of her attention, as she would be of his. But it would take work and discipline. And prayer.

She prayed right then that God would help her put Scott in the past once and for all. She thanked Him for the brief months she had spent with him and for the wonder he had brought to her life, but she asked that God would fill her mind and heart with the deep feelings for Jim that attracted her to him in the first place.

Suddenly, she was nervous. The church was stifling with the windows and curtains open, but no breeze. Her watch read almost twelve, and she knew the humidity was in the nineties and the temperature probably higher than that.

Her father and mother tried in vain to talk her into going to lunch with them before coming back to get ready. "There's a nice restaurant at our hotel," her father said.

"I know," she said. "That's one of the reasons I chose it for you. You go and enjoy a leisurely lunch. By the time you're done and freshen up, it'll be time to come back here."

Jennifer was amazed at how long it took the church to empty after the morning service. It was almost one o'clock by the time the pastor, Reverend Howell Cass, had shaken the last hand, listened to the last suggestion, smiled the second to last smile, and called his wife to tell her he was almost on his way home. She had imperceptibly slipped from his side a half hour before to get dinner on the table at the parsonage.

When Jennifer and Candy ducked into a back room for a final check of the fit of the bridal gown, Pastor Cass started from the back pew and worked his way slowly to the front, straightening the hymnals, replacing the pencils, replenishing the information cards, and picking up scraps of paper and works of art by four-year-old illustrators.

A few minutes later, with Jennifer in her gown and stocking feet, working on her veil, he knocked gently. "Excuse me," he said, as Candy opened the door. "Oh, my, Jennifer, you look radiant. Just beautiful." And he offered the last smile necessary before the ceremony that afternoon. "Need anything?"

6   Jennifer Grey Mysteries

"Just a sedative," she joked. "No, we're fine."

"A couple of carloads just pulled up," he said. "One full of your friends, I think. The other's the florist's van. I'll point them your way. And my office is unlocked in case you need to use the phone."

"What a sweet man to have for a pastor," Candy said when he had gone.

Jennifer nodded absently, something in the back of her mind telling her that Candy was right, that she did have a wonderful pastor and that she was fortunate. But her mind was elsewhere. She heard the giggling of her attendants as they bantered with the pastor, and she felt the stifling heat and discomfort from the exertion of having put her wedding dress on too early.

"I'm not going to sit around in this thing," she said.

Candy nodded. "I should say not. You ought to sit by the fan in your slip for a few minutes and cool off." She helped Jennifer out of her dress. And Candy was right; the fan felt good until her body was no longer fooled by the slight difference in temperature caused by the air blowing on her perspiring skin. Then she was hot again. And her friends were filing into the room, giving her quick hugs, oohing and aahing over the dress as Candy held it up to show them. And the phone was ringing in the pastor's office.

"I've got to try my dress on right now," one of the girls said. "I think I've gained five pounds since I finished it." She stepped out of her shorts and top. "Should someone answer that phone?"

"Nah. The pastor'll get it."

"Is he still here?"

"I don't think so."

"Yes, he is. Oh, somebody got it."

There was a knock at the door. "Jennifer," came the voice of the pastor. "Jim's on the phone. Didn't sound like him, but you know what wedding days do to grooms."

"Could you tell him I'll be a minute, or can I call him somewhere?"

"I told him you might be a minute and that I was leaving. I really must go."

"Thanks!" She turned to the other girls. "Any men out there in the hall?"

"Yeah. The florist and a custodian."

"Oh, great!"

"Here, wear my shorts and top to run to the phone."

Jennifer jumped into the slightly baggy substitutes and hurried to the pastor's office. "Hi, darling," she said, the phone to her ear.

"Excuse me, ma'am, but this is Jim McGraw at The Consulate. Your mother asked that I phone you to tell you that your father has become ill."

Jennifer held her breath. "Ill?" she managed. "What do you mean, ill?"

Veiled Threat

7

"He's apparently had a heart attack, ma'am."

"Where have they taken him?"

"Well, he's still here, Miss Grey. I think you might want to come quickly."

"Is he alive?"

Jennifer panicked at the pause she detected from the other end. "I believe he is, ma'am. But I would suggest you hurry."

Jennifer hung up, fighting tears. *I should have gone with them to lunch the way they wanted, she thought. It's too much, a wedding, this weather, the trip. But he's always been so healthy.*

Jennifer ran down the hall, hoping to pour out to Candy her need to get to the hotel. But the room was empty. The girls had moved into a restroom down the hall, so she just scribbled on a blackboard, *Candy, Dad may have had a heart attack. Will call you. Jenn.* She grabbed her purse, stepped into someone else's casual canvas slip-ons, and ran to the car. She could call Candy and the pastor from the hotel, and someone could get a message to Jim. He would understand that there couldn't be a wedding today. If only he could be with her now.

She didn't even have time to feel silly. She had pulled up her slip and stuffed it into the baggy shorts and wore nylons with someone else's shoes. She dug for her keys as she slid behind the wheel, and the vinyl seat burned her legs.

The wheel was hot to the touch, as was the ignition. She rolled her window down and started the car, cranking up the air conditioner at the same time. Normally she would have sat in the steaming car until it cooled down some, but now gravel and dust spit from under the rear wheels as she pulled the black sports car around the side of the church.

She braked quickly at the street, reminding herself that she was a good half hour from the hotel, even at top speed. She turned left, barely noticing the florist's van parked in front until she was about forty feet from it and accelerating. A dark-complexioned young man with curly black hair and a walrus moustache stepped out from behind it, skipped across the street into her path, and raised his arms.

All Jennifer could do was hit the brakes and jerk the wheel to the right, sending her into a broadside skid that just missed the man and left her perpendicular to the street on the grassy shoulder. In the microsecond since she'd just missed him, Jennifer thought about honking and yelling, and even about the irony of running a man down on the day of her wedding, which would be postponed by her father's heart attack. Emotionally, she was ready to burst.

8   Jennifer Grey Mysteries

She looked left and turned the wheel, but before she could gun the engine again, the young man shouted, "I heard about your father! Are you going to see him?"

The incongruity of it didn't hit her at first. Who could have told him? How could he have known? Who was he anyway? "Yes!" she shouted, as he slowed to walk in front of the car. She was dumbfounded. She just sat and watched as he came around to the passenger's side and opened the door. He wore a loose-fitting smock that made her assume he was with the florists and also made her find room in her boggled mind to wonder if he was very hot because of it.

"I'm going with you," he said, smiling and shutting the car door.

Jennifer put her foot on the brake. "You are not!" she said. "Now get out and let me—"

He reached over with his left hand and placed a long, smooth finger on her lips. With his right hand he reached down into the left side of his smock and produced an ugly, stubby weapon Jennifer recognized immediately. An Uzi, the same piece carried by the Secret Service men who guard the President, pound for pound, one of the most powerful weapons on earth.

As if reading her mind, the young man cradled the Uzi over his left forearm, aimed at her rib cage, out of sight of anyone driving by. "It will chew you up and spit you out and leave your body in neat little rows next to what's left of your car door," he said. "You wanna start drivin'?"

"Where?"

"Pershing, south of the Stevenson."

"Pershing is north of the Stevenson."

"Not east of Pulaski, it's not," he said.

"What's this all about?"

"No questions."

"You picked the wrong person then, pal. All I do is ask questions. Start with my father."

"Your father is fine."

"Are you sure?"

"You know better than we do. We only saw him at The Consulate to make sure everything would work. We got no problem with your father."

"You've got a problem with me?"

"Not if you cooperate."

"How come I feel like I'm in a B-movie?"

"You're gonna feel like you're in a casket if you don't step on it."

"C'mon, who are you, and what's so important that you need to scare the life out of me and kidnap me on my wedding day?"

"We need you, that's all. Or I should say, we need your audience. I'm Benito Diaz, and you're under arrest by the Guest Workers Party of the Estados Unidos Mexicanos."

Jennifer shook her head and pressed her lips together. "That's just Spanish for United Mexican States," she said. "Mexico. What's your problem?"

"You got a smart mouth, lady," Diaz said. "Shut up till we get where we're goin'. Then you can ask whatever you want." He turned in the seat and rapped on Jennifer's luggage with his free hand. "Honeymoon stuff, huh?"

She nodded.

"Good. You're gonna need clothes. We're gonna be spending a lotta time together."

Two

Ricardo DiPietro and his family had been handling the floral arrangements at Chicago city and suburban weddings for decades. "And we've never lost anything off the truck before," he told Edwin Hines, the church custodian.

"What'd you lose?" Hines asked, his lined face showing deep concern. "I'm sure it wasn't any of our people."

"Oh, sure!" DiPietro said. "It's *never* church people!"

"I'm sure we'll be happy to replace whatever it is you lost," Hines said.

"Oh, it's just my son Richie's smock, that's all. But I saw him lay it across the bumper myself, and I don't like the idea of somebody messin' with my truck."

"I'm sorry."

"You got anyone who can keep an eye on it for me, or do I hafta lock it up?"

"You'd better lock it up."

"Then I'm gonna park it back here and unload a lot of the big stuff. Is there a room back here we can use?"

"I think the girls are dressing back here, but I'll ask."

Ed Hines knocked, then opened the door carefully when no one answered and he heard no activity. "The bridal gown is in here," he told the florist, "so at least the bride will be coming back to dress here."

"No, she won't," Candy said, approaching from behind the men and slipping into the room. "We found a better spot downstairs. Anyway, I have to do a little work on that dress." She gathered it up carefully. "Is Jennifer still on the phone? Could you point her our way?"

"Sure," Mr. Hines said. "Do you know if the men will be wanting to dress in here?"

"Don't think so. They're in another room downstairs."

She hurried out.

"Then I don't see why you can't use this room," Hines told DiPietro. He turned the blackboard toward the wall. "Let me just get this out of the way, and you can slide all those chairs into one corner if you want to."

10

Veiled Threat   11

"Thanks, man," the florist said. "I don't wanna be no trouble. I just don't wanna get robbed blind either. Richie!" he shouted out the door. "Bring the truck around back, and carry the candelabra in through here."

In the hall, Hines met Jim Purcell. He was wearing cutoff jeans and a sleeveless sweatshirt. Except for the tux in a plastic bag slung over his shoulder, he looked as if he was ready for a game of basketball. But he was also nervous.

"The bride isn't around here anywhere, is she?" he asked.

"On the phone in the pastor's office, I think," the janitor told him.

"Don't let me see her," Jim said, grinning sheepishly and heading for the stairs. Hines waited until Jim was out of sight before peeking into the pastor's office. It was empty. He shrugged and hoped bride and groom wouldn't run into each other before they wanted to.

Jennifer's fast-food lunch grew cold as the other girls wolfed theirs down and began to get dressed. In her long gown and bare feet, Candy skipped upstairs and poked her head into the dressing room turned florist headquarters. The busy DiPietro family hardly had time to look up.

"Anybody seen the bride?" Candy asked.

Several shook their heads. "I saw Mr. Hines with the groom near the pastor's office a little while ago," Mr. DiPietro said.

Candy nodded. *That must be where they are, then,* she decided. But as the parking lot filled with cars and the photographer came asking for the bride, Candy and the other girls grew nervous. Finally, she was selected to interrupt the couple in the pastor's office.

When she found it empty, she enlisted a few more people, and they went scurrying about the church in search of the missing bride. As a last resort, Candy rapped on the men's dressing room door. "Anybody know where Jim and—"

The door opened and there stood Jim in tux trousers, cumberbund, and loose bow tie. "I, uh, I was just looking for one of the girls," Candy said.

"No girls in here," Jim said. "Just us chickens. Who's missin?"

"We'll find her," Candy said, hiding her concern. She found Ed Hines briefing Pastor Cass, who had just arrived, on the arrangements. "Excuse me, Ed," Candy said, "but did you tell Jennifer we had moved downstairs?"

"I'm sorry, Candy, but I haven't seen Jennifer since she took the phone call."

"Me either," the pastor said, smiling. "Don't imagine she's hiding somewhere, do you? A little case of cold feet?"

"Hardly," Candy said. "I know her better than that."

12   **Jennifer Grey Mysteries**

"I do too," the pastor said, quickly sobered to Candy's seriousness. "Well, listen, there aren't that many places to hide here. I'm sure she'll turn up. If we see her, we'll send her to you. You know, I recall a wedding where the bride and groom sneaked into the balcony and watched the preliminaries together, getting into their respective positions just in time for the processional."

"But Jim is accounted for," Candy said. "I didn't tell him that Jennifer wasn't."

"I'm sure there's some logical explanation," the pastor said. "It'll seem quite silly an hour from now."

"I hope so," Candy said, a feeling of dread washing over her.

The three unsuccessful searchers got back together. "Is her car here?"

"She wouldn't have gone anywhere."

"Better check."

"What's she driving?"

"A black Firebird with the back loaded. You can't miss it."

A minute later the scout returned. "Only two Firebirds in the lot. Neither is black."

"I can't believe it," Candy said. "Why wouldn't she have said something? Could it be a prank?"

"Yeah, that's it! A joke. Someone talked her into running out for a Coke and is making her sweat getting back in time."

Candy looked doubtful. "That's not Jennifer," she concluded. "She'd never put up with it."

"Then what could it be, Can? She chickening out?"

"No way. That's not how she'd do it. She'd talk to Jim. Anyway, it's out of the question. There hasn't been one hint of that. Anyway, I just talked to Jim, and he was his usual self. If there had been some discussion about calling the whole thing off, he sure wasn't in on it and doesn't know anything about it."

"But didn't she take a call from him a little while ago?"

"That's what I thought, but I didn't want to ask Jim. There's no sense worrying him about this until we have to."

A woman knocked and opened the door a few inches. "Places," she called out in a singsong voice.

"Um, ma'am," Candy called after her. "Could you stall the organist for a few minutes? Jennifer needs a little more time."

"Oh! Well, I'll see what I can do. Do hurry though."

As soon as she was gone, all the attendants got in on the discussion with Candy.

"Then what? Something came up? She had to leave for some reason?"

"Obviously."

Veiled Threat   13

"But what could it have been? And why wouldn't she have told one of us or the pastor or at least left a note?"

"Maybe she did," Candy said. "It was while she was on the phone that we moved out of the upstairs room. Maybe there's a note in the pastor's office."

"Or in the first room we were in."

"Let's look."

On their way up the stairs they were met by the same woman. She was carrying Jennifer's wedding dress and was nearly in tears. "Here's the dress, but where's the bride?" she whined.

"Uh, we're not sure," Candy said. "We need a little more time."

"Oh, my. Oh, no!"

"Did you stall the organist?"

"Yes. He's going to play three more pieces. That might give you ten minutes. But where is she?"

"We don't know! Can you find the pastor for us?"

Without a word, the woman scurried away. The attendants, their hems gathered at their knees, continued up the stairs to the pastor's office. It was empty, and there was no note. As they hurried down the hall to the original dressing room, they passed the groomsmen.

"Thought you were supposed to come in from the foyer," one of them said. And Jim squinted solemnly, apparently wondering where Jennifer was and what was going on.

"We will," Candy said on the way by, as if the men should mind their own business.

She opened the door to the back room, and the rest of the girls followed her in to where the DiPietros were packing up.

"We'll be back to pick up the stuff from the sanctuary later," Mr. DiPietro said to Candy, as if she cared. "As soon as we put this room back the way we found it, we'll be outta here."

"Don't mind us," Candy said. "We're just looking for a note someone might have left us."

"Didn't see nothing like that," Mr. DiPietro said. His son backed out the rear exit with several empty boxes and rolls of crepe paper while his wife gathered up pin cushions and leftover bunting.

As Candy looked under books and papers for any sign of a note, another girl found Jennifer's Sunday clothes, as well as her going away clothes. "Jennifer either left in her slip or she's wearing my stuff, which she wore to the phone and which I don't see anywhere."

The pastor entered. "Still no bride?" he asked, no longer amused by the situation.

14   Jennifer Grey Mysteries

Candy shook her head. "And her car's gone. No one has seen her since she took the phone call. And no one saw her leave either."

"It's past time for the ceremony," Pastor Cass said. "I'm going to have to say something to the people."

"But there's nothing to say yet, is there?"

He shook his head, the look in his eyes making clear that his mind was working on something. But nothing was coming together for him. Mr. DiPietro enlisted his son's help in rearranging the chairs, then putting the blackboard back where they had found it.

The DiPietros ignored the writing on it, assuming it was Sunday school stuff. But as they left with an inane wish for good luck in finding the bride, the message Jennifer left for Candy stared the women and the pastor in the face.

Candy dropped into a chair and hid her face in her hands. "Why wouldn't she have at least told Jim?" someone asked.

"She probably expected me to," Candy said, her words muffled by her fingers. "And I'd better do it quick."

The woman with Jennifer's dress burst into the room. "The men were supposed to wait for you, Pastor," she said, "but the guests were getting restless. We let the men go out. You'd better catch up with them."

"I'm afraid Jim's going to have to find out about this along with everyone else," the pastor said. The girls followed him and peeked through a side door to the platform as he strode to the center.

The overhead fans were working overtime, accomplishing little more than moving the hot air around. People were fanning themselves with bulletins, wedding programs, even hymnals. But mostly they were murmuring among themselves about why the groomsmen had come out before the pastor and craning their necks to see where the bridesmaids might be.

"Wait a minute!" Candy whispered to the other girls. "Isn't that Mrs. Knight in the front row?"

The others crowded for a better look. "I don't know," one said. "It's been years."

"It is her!" another said.

"Ladies and gentlemen," the pastor began. "I'm sorry to report that the bride has been called away unexpectedly due to a sudden illness in the family." He held up a hand to silence the collective gasp. Lillian Knight lurched in her seat and turned around to seek out her husband, who was waiting in the foyer for Jennifer and the bridesmaids. He scanned the second and third rows behind his wife to be sure that his son and other daughter and their children were all accounted for.

Veiled Threat

Jim's eyes darted to his future mother-in-law, then to Mr. Knight, who shrugged.

"We don't know how serious the problem is at this moment," the pastor continued, "but apparently Mr. Knight, Jennifer Grey's father, has fallen ill. This will mean a postponement of the ceremony, and I would suggest that before we leave, we all bow and pray that—"

"Hold on a second!" Mr. Knight shouted, charging briskly up the aisle. "I'm right here, and I'm fine. What's going on?"

As the guests chattered and some even laughed—assuming the announcement was a cover for a bride who had changed her mind—Jim left his position and huddled with the pastor and Mr. and Mrs. Knight.

"What's the deal?" Jim asked. "Where is she?"

Reverend Cass told the three quickly of the note on the blackboard and of the fact that Jennifer had apparently left in her own car, leaving her wedding dress, Sunday clothes, and honeymoon outfit behind. "I want to see the note," Jim said, signaling Detective Sergeant Ellis Milton—one of his groomsmen—to join him. "Don't let anyone touch it."

"Take the men back," the pastor advised, "and Mr. and Mrs. Knight, if you'd just take your seats in the front row for a moment." Mrs. Knight complied. Mr. Knight did not. He followed the groomsmen to the back.

"I'm sorry about the confusion," the pastor announced. "It's clear we are not entirely sure what has happened, but the bride is not here, and until further notice, there will not be a wedding today."

Three

If the ornery-looking Uzi hadn't convinced her, the dumping of her less-than-a-year old car into Lake Michigan made Jennifer realize that she was in mortal danger.

What amazed her was the cool aplomb with which Benito Diaz, if that was indeed his real name, arranged for the dumping. He had directed her to drive to a secluded alcove at the beach, several miles south of where a thousand people were swimming and sunbathing.

"Pull up next to that van," he had said.

"You mean the green panel truck?"

"Call it whatever you want, Jennifer," he said, and she wished he hadn't used her first name. There was something distasteful about being on a first-name basis with a terrorist.

Terrorist. It was the first time she had allowed herself to mentally articulate it. But that's what he was. Even if he appeared in his early twenties at most, and even if the walrus moustache was the only hair he had seemed to be able to cultivate on his smooth, dark face. She wondered if a terrorist so young and with such delicate hands and slim, long fingers had the intestinal fortitude to use the ugly weapon he brandished. Or was he a complete phony, masquerading without even ammunition? Could the weapon be a fake? A toy store special? She remembered the cold steel in her ribs in front of the church and knew she was kidding herself.

"Good," Diaz said. "Now pull around the other side of him, and park as close to him as you can."

Jennifer shot him a double take. The panel truck was situated out on a concrete pier and was parked parallel with the water, seemingly at the edge of the pier. As she pulled around the far side, she realized that there was just enough room for her car and maybe a foot or two to open her door.

"I should take a hard right and see who survives," Jennifer said, staring coldly at Diaz and edging as close to the side of the pier as she dared. She probably cleared it by four inches, but from the driver's side it seemed that half the car was over the water.

16

Veiled Threat

Apparently the effect wasn't much different from Diaz's perspective. "Hey!" he shouted, involuntarily leaning toward her, as if to keep the car from rolling into the drink.

"Scared?" she asked.

That had angered him. She was only dimly aware that the driver's side door on the other side of the panel truck had opened and shut, because the fire in Benito's black eyes burned into her own.

He raised the automatic weapon and pressed it against her right cheekbone, pushing her head back until it hit the window. He kept pushing until she winced in pain. "You're hurting me," she said softly.

He swore. "I'll kill you if you try to mess with me," he said. "You're worth nothing to me!"

She tried to nod, but the steel against her flesh paralyzed her from the neck up. Jennifer wanted to reach up and tear at the Mexican's eyes with her long fingernails, but he had finally gotten through to her. She believed him. He would kill her.

There was a soft knock on the window near her head, and Diaz slowly lessened the pressure on her face until she could turn to look. In the small area she had left between her car and the truck stood a taller, leaner, older, more Indian-looking man she assumed was also a Mexican.

"Roll the window down," Diaz said. "I want to introduce you to Luis Cardenas."

"What do you want me to do, shake his hand?" she said, tempering the sarcasm only slightly.

"Exactly."

But she didn't offer her hand. Cardenas, his weathered face eyeing her warily, put a hand through the window. Jennifer ignored it until she felt the Uzi on her cheek again. Then she raised her right hand to meet Cardenas's, but didn't squeeze when their hands met. Strangely, Cardenas didn't either.

"Pleased to meet you, señora," he said in an accent so thick it made Diaz sound like an Ivy Leaguer. She was amazed at the homework they had done. How could they know she was technically a married woman, being a widow, and that "señora" was indeed the correct address? Or had it been an insignificant lucky guess?

"Leave it in neutral and turn the engine off," Diaz instructed. "Then get out."

"You first," Jennifer said, wondering why she was motivated to be so smart with her captor.

"You have a wild one, Benito," Cardenas said, laughing. There was no way Diaz could get out on his own side without tumbling into the lake. He

18 Jennifer Grey Mysteries

just stared at her. She shifted into neutral, turned off the ignition, and started to remove the keys.

"Leave them there," Diaz said. Jennifer stepped out and thought about slamming the door as he slid across the seat behind her. Cardenas awkwardly shuffled out of the way, and the three of them barely fit between the vehicles.

The shorter man tucked his weapon into his pants and leaned in the window to wrench the wheel hard, all the way to the right. Jennifer had not seen Cardenas's weapon yet and found herself looking for someplace to run. But there was nowhere to go. The pier was at least a quarter mile long, and even if they couldn't catch her on foot, there was plenty of time to run her down with the truck.

Cardenas opened the passenger-side door of the truck and motioned that Jennifer should climb in. "You can see from here," he said. When he shut the door and turned around, she saw a .45 automatic pistol wedged into the back of his pants.

The two men, whom she could now see were at least a foot apart in height, emptied the luggage from her car and piled it into the back of the truck. Then they pushed the Firebird from behind. The right front tire dropped off the side first, and the crunch of metal onto concrete sickened Jennifer.

Her car, the beautifully designed and fully appointed style she had been able to justify and afford only when her column became one of the most widely syndicated in the country, sat with its right front tire off the edge of a pier, the left rear off the pavement, and the undercarriage crumpled under its own weight against the cement.

The men counted aloud in unison in Spanish and heaved again at the back bumper, causing the left front tire to also drop off the edge. The left rear bumper creased the truck as the car turned toward the water, but now it was hung up, the front tires clear of the pier, the back tires only barely touching the ground, and the main weight of the car resting on the edge of the concrete.

Both men stood back and took deep breaths. "*Uno mas*," Cardenas said, and he bent to the task again. They pushed and heaved and rocked, and the car lurched and scraped and inched until the weight of the engine was fully past the fulcrum of the pier, and the car's own momentum carried it clear of the pavement.

Jennifer could hardly believe the splash made by the short drop into the water. It couldn't have been two feet, but the water leaped at least twelve feet into the air, and a wave cascaded up over the pier, causing Cardenas and Diaz to dance back toward the truck.

Veiled Threat 19

They both entered from the driver's side, first the taller, older man, who disconcertingly sat directly behind Jennifer where she couldn't see him. He tossed the keys to Diaz, who fired up the engine and impetuously reached over and pinched Jennifer's cheek lightly. He winked at her and smiled as if he had just pulled off the greatest high school prank in history.

She turned away and stared out the window. "We could have just as easily left you in the car," he said. And she knew it was true. She breathed a silent prayer of thanks, wondering where this was all leading, when and where it would end, and how soon she would be reunited with Jim.

Within fifteen minutes, Benito Diaz pulled into a garage at the back of a dingy, two story, redbrick building near the northeast corner of Pershing and Kedzie, in the shadow of the Stevenson Expressway.

Jennifer forced herself to drink in every sight and sound. She didn't know what these people wanted or what they expected, but she had the feeling she would need to employ every detail-oriented bone in her body if she had any hope of escaping.

A heavy metal overhead door rose and fell automatically as the truck passed through. As Jennifer's eyes slowly grew accustomed to the darkness inside, the threshold seemed to have worked magic on her captors' manners. They were suddenly deferential, almost to the point of being sickening. They treated her like a lady, opening the door of the truck for her, carrying her luggage, speaking softly, calling her Mrs. Grey.

She didn't know what to make of it, and while she was still determined to drink in every inch and every sound of her new surroundings, she was—she finally allowed herself to realize—weak with hunger.

And fear. She couldn't deny it. She wanted to be tough, once the initial shock wore off. She had been so relieved that her father was all right that she had enjoyed a brief—and false—sense of well-being, the feeling that nothing could really go too terribly wrong.

But the cold steel in her ribs, the Uzi barrel in her face, her car in the lake, the entombing of the truck in the secluded, yet apparently well-equipped building, and the disconcerting turn to politeness by her captors gave her a sinking, almost helplessly hopeless feeling of dread.

Neither Cardenas nor Diaz had mentioned anything about anyone else being involved in her abduction, but Jennifer sensed such a feeling of anticipation in both men all along the way that their sudden personality change was the only further clue she needed. She was about to meet whomever else was behind this scheme, probably the mind that had conceived the plot.

She was eager to meet him or her and to find out, if possible, how the Guest Workers—or whatever it was they called themselves—knew so much about her and her parents' arrangements. She wondered who had

20   **Jennifer Grey Mysteries**

placed the phony call purported to be from The Consulate Hotel. She wondered how Benito Diaz had gotten to her church. And she wondered if they would have any food.

Diaz and Cardenas pointed up a back staircase with a single light bulb burning at the top. When Jennifer reached a multi-locked door upstairs, she stopped. The two men stood on either side of her and moved close, as if they had a secret.

Diaz affected a heavy Spanish accent, easily as thick as Cardenas's, and it made Jennifer wonder if the latter's was phony too. "You are about to meet Adolpho Alvarez, our boss, and Maria Ruiz, his wife. We call him Double-A or A-A, but you will do well to call him Mr. Alvarez or Señor Alvarez."

What if I don't want to call him anything? Jennifer wondered. But she wasn't about to cause trouble now.

From inside the door she heard a female voice with a flat midwestern accent. "Benito?"

"Si!"

"Luis?"

"Si!"

"Mission accomplished?"

"Si!"

Several locks began to pop open, and the door swung in. Jennifer was almost startled by the striking, smiling face of Maria Ruiz. It was so jarring and so unlike what she might have expected that she almost smiled back. It was the way Jennifer had been raised to be polite, to smile when smiled at, to speak when spoken to. Jennifer wondered how such a delicately featured woman, apparently about her own age, could be involved in a terrorist organization.

"Welcome to the temporary headquarters of the Guest Workers Party of the United Mexican States," Maria said, extending her hand. Jennifer had to check herself to keep from reaching for it. Maria Ruiz never flinched. "Can you smell lunch?"

Jennifer nodded, wondering if perhaps she should have returned the handshake to be certain of getting some food. She was light-headed, having skipped breakfast. "My husband is the best Mexican cook I have ever seen," Maria said.

And Jennifer *could* smell it. She was able to pick out the fragrances of the slowly melting cheese, the flour and corn tortillas, the refried beans, the rice, even the guacamole. She envisioned tacos and enchiladas and burritos.

Veiled Threat

Still smiling, her even white teeth gleaming against the darkness of her face, Maria looked deep into Jennifer's eyes. "It is what we will all enjoy, if you cooperate. It is what four of us will enjoy if you do not."

Jennifer wanted to promise anything at that point, but she had established a smart mouth with Diaz and Cardenas, and already a cool distance from Maria. She feared she might be misguided, but she thought she should be consistent, in case that posture proved to be a strength. If it cost her a meal, however, she would have to rethink it.

Maria led her into what appeared to be a nicely furnished apartment. It was carpeted and decorated in a conventionally American way. In fact, aside from the aroma from the kitchen and the clothes of the three she had met so far, there would have been no hint of anything Mexican or Spanish about the place.

The strange thing about the large living room, with its television and couches and chairs, was that it had no windows. It was well-lighted and cozy, but somewhat claustrophobic. A huge wall air conditioner blasted icy air throughout the place with such power that Jennifer's hair danced in its wake.

Maria pointed to one end of a huge sofa, and Jennifer lowered herself carefully. She was tired, exhausted, having transferred her nervous excitement about the wedding to this fear for her life. "Adolpho will be right in," Maria said. "Please do not speak to him unless he speaks to you."

"I may not even then," Jennifer said, almost casually, surprising even herself. Diaz and Cardenas looked at each other and at Maria, and they all smiled knowingly. The men took Jennifer's luggage into another room, and she noted the loud knocking of the lanky Luis's cowboy boots on the hardwood hallway between the carpeted rooms.

When Benito and Luis returned, they detoured through the kitchen, and each carried in two large pitchers of beer. They set them on a coffee table in front of Jennifer and Maria. "You like?" Luis asked, smiling. Jennifer shook her head. "Somethin' else?" he asked, as if she had dropped in after church. Which, she realized, she had.

"Anything else," she said, hoping he knew she meant anything other than whisky or wine. He came back with a two-liter bottle of cola, which almost made her smile. It was so perfect and seemed so out of place.

From the kitchen Jennifer heard the low, rumbling voice of Adolpho Alvarez, who bellowed his wife's name with an accent. Maria jumped and hurried to the kitchen, returning a minute later with five large drinking glasses. She was pouring the beer for herself and the three men when Alvarez entered with a tray piled high with hot Mexican delights.

Jennifer almost studied the food before the man, but he was an imposing figure. Almost six feet tall, Adolpho was wide and stocky and muscled

22   Jennifer Grey Mysteries

with long, black hair and a square jaw. She guessed him at least in his late thirties.

"The joke among my people," he said, "is that Americanos think our food is spicy. In truth, it is very bland—lots of bread, little salt. You season to taste." He smiled, displaying a silver eyetooth on the right, and produced several small saucers of hot sauce from the heaping tray.

Only Jennifer and Maria sat on the couch. Benito dragged a chair over to one end of the coffee table for Adolpho, then sat on the floor next to Luis, directly across from the women.

Without any amenities or any more talk—let alone any plates—the four dug into the treats. Adolpho sat on the edge of his chair and leaned forward. Gingerly picking up a steaming flauta, he cocked his head so as not to spill anything, laid one end across his tongue, and devoured half the flauta in one bite.

The others tore at beans and rice and guacamole with a fork each, their only utensils. Jennifer sat with her hands in her lap. Her mouth watered. Her heart raced.

Four

It was the first time anyone in the church, from the pastor to the organist to the groomsmen and bridesmaids and family and friends, had ever been involved in a wedding that didn't come off on schedule. Anyone, that is, except the florist.

Ricardo DiPietro shook his head and smiled as several hundred people filed out the back past his truck. Usually, he was long gone by the time the occasions broke up, and he, like most others, merely felt that the groom had been jilted, left standing at the altar.

"Happens all the time," he said to whomever would listen, not thinking that he attended several weddings a week and that the odds were better that he would have witnessed something similar. "I saw a guy leave a girl at the altar and come back later and talk the priest into marryin' him to one of the bridesmaids. Brought two witnesses. Just them and us in the big church with all the trimmings. Saw another one where a guy stood up when they asked if anybody had an objection. He said he did because the girl had told him the night before that she loved him but couldn't get out of the marriage. The minister handled it pretty well, I thought. Told the congregation he was going to give the girl one chance to publicly confirm or deny the story. She said it was true, and the pastor said he couldn't perform the wedding. Don't know if she married either one of the saps. I got paid for the flowers, that's all I know. Whether the wedding comes off is none of my concern. If the flowers are there, somebody pays. That's it."

Inside, there was a crowd on the platform that wouldn't have been bigger if the wedding had taken place as usual. The men and women in the wedding party were chattering, Mr. and Mrs. Knight were there, the pastor, the janitor, the woman with Jennifer's dress, all of them.

Jim pulled his best man, Detective Ellis Milton, to the side. The swarthy, thick investigator was sweating profusely. "Ellis, I need you, man," Jim said. "Can you handle this? I'm at a loss."

"I'll do whatever I can, Jimmy," the fast-talking Ellis said. "But we've gotta break up this crowd, find out who knows what, and get an order of events. Can you get me a notebook and something to write with?"

24   Jennifer Grey Mysteries

Relieved to have a chore, anything to do that would allow him to worry without having the responsibility for the investigation, Jim ran to the pastor.

"I need paper and pen for Detective Milton, and I need to let everyone know that he's in charge. Whatever he says goes."

"Fair enough," Pastor Cass said, nodding to Ed Hines who came up with a notebook and a pen for Ellis Milton.

Ellis loosened his tie and took off his tweed jacket, shedding also the cumberbund and slipping the suspender straps off his shoulders. The rest of the men immediately followed suit. "Could we all sit here in the first row or two?" he asked, exhibiting enough authority in his voice that everyone fell silent and complied.

"Now, I hate to be cold," Ellis began, "because I know you all care and are concerned. But if you did not see Jennifer between the end of the church service this morning and the time she disappeared, I need you to leave."

There were several groans from the groomsmen and the bridesmaids. "I know Jim and Jennifer will call you as soon as we get to the bottom of this, but you have to understand that if you have nothing substantial to contribute, you're going to be in the way. Do us all a favor and just go somewhere—out for dinner or home or wherever you want. I'm sorry, but I must insist."

Several stood to reluctantly step out. "What about me?" Mr. Knight asked. "Lil and I saw Jenn right after the service and tried to talk her into going to lunch with us." His voice nearly broke. "I wish she'd come with us."

"But she didn't, and that's the last you saw of her, and the first you knew she was missing was just now, right?"

The Knights nodded. Ellis had bad news for them. There was nothing they could do then and there. He searched his mind for a diplomatic way to get rid of them. "What I want to do," he said, "is to pick up the sequence from there, and I need only those persons who saw or talked to Jennifer after that. Mr. and Mrs. Knight, the most important thing you can do is go back to your hotel, in case Jennifer or whoever she's with tries to get in touch with you."

Mrs. Knight stood and began moving into the aisle. But her husband, the big, white-haired, independent father of the missing bride, remained seated and stared at the detective. Ellis just stared back, trying with all that was in him to look firm yet compassionate, urgent but not panicky, insistent but not insensitive. Finally, the father stood to leave. "We're at The Consulate," he said. "Don't hesitate to call."

"Thank you. Anybody talk to Jennifer earlier?"

Veiled Threat 25

"I did," Candy said. "I called her early this morning. Just to see how she was. I was curious, I admit it. Just wanted to see what a nervous bride sounded like. She wasn't nervous at all. Not harried—nothing. Same as ever. I had my own church to go to this morning, and when I got here, she was in the back, just waiting for help to get into her dress."

"It must not have been too long after that that I saw her," the pastor said. "As I recall, she was in her wedding dress, but was without shoes or veil. She said something funny, I think, but I don't remember exactly what it was."

"Something about needing a sedative," Candy said. "Wasn't that when you told her she had a phone call?"

"No, that wasn't until after the other girls got here."

"Oh, you're right," Candy said, "because Jenn borrowed someone else's clothes to run to the phone."

"That must have been at least a half hour after I saw her the first time," he said. "Maybe longer. In fact, I didn't see her the second time, I assume, because she was dressing or something. I was on my way out the door when I got the call from you, Jim."

Jim flinched. "From *me*? I didn't call here today, Howell, excuse me, Pastor Cass. Did the person say he was me?"

"Well, he said *Jim*, and I just assumed. He referred to Jennifer by Jenn, I think, and so, like I say, I assumed."

"But Pastor," Candy reminded him, "you said something to Jennifer through the door about it not sounding like Jim."

"That's right! I didn't think it sounded like him. But I still thought it was him because who else would be calling here, and who knows what a wedding day might do to a man's voice? Anyway, whoever it was didn't say much. Just, 'Hi, Pastor, this is Jim. Is Jenn there?' You can see how I assumed—"

"I sure can," Ellis said. "It's obvious already we're dealing with someone who's done some homework. What were the odds the pastor would answer the phone, as opposed to the custodian?"

"One in two," Edwin Hines said. "We would have been the only two men here at the time, and in fact, I don't think I was here that early."

"You were," Pastor Cass said. "You got here just as I was leaving."

Ellis Milton looked at Jim out of the corner of his eye. "The caller could have been someone who had already been in proximity of the church," he said. "Could have been calling from nearby."

"Or got a tip from someone nearby," Jim said. "Someone who told him the pastor was in or near his office."

Ellis nodded. "So Jennifer borrowed someone's clothes?"

26   Jennifer Grey Mysteries

"Mine," a bridesmaid said. "And they were a little too big for her."

"So she's wearing slightly baggy clothes. What did they look like?"

"Red long-sleeved top and khaki shorts."

"Would she have been barefoot?"

"When she left us she was," Candy said. "But my beige canvas slip-ons are missing from the back room now, so she may have put them on to go to her car."

"And if she took her own car," Jim said, "you can forget looking for her by her clothes. She planned on taking a lot of stuff with her. Several pieces of luggage."

There were several dejected nods. "Any chance she'd have left of her own accord?" Ellis asked.

"Ellis!" Jim scolded.

"I have to ask, Jim. She was here one minute and gone the next."

"Yeah, but we also know there was a bogus phone call, and she left a note. If she was going to run out on me, she wouldn't have had to invent anything."

Ellis leaned back against the piano and folded his arms across his chest. "So, our hypothesis at this point is that she was tricked by a caller into believing that her father had had a heart attack, and we have to assume it was supposedly at his hotel or en route, because it made her want to leave immediately, even without telling anyone. Pretty risky of the pranksters."

"How do you mean?" Jim asked.

"How did they know she would come out alone? Wouldn't it have been logical for him or her or them to assume that she would be surrounded by girl friends at that moment? Wouldn't the natural thing be for her to tell the girls and have one or two of them go with her, maybe even drive her, maybe in one of their cars?"

No one said anything. "I can't make it make sense either," Jim offered finally. "There's just so much we don't know."

"Jim, do you feel up to helping out?"

"I have to do something."

"Then call downtown and have a detail assigned to The Consulate. See if they had a medical emergency this afternoon and whether they could have called the wrong contact person by mistake. I'm assuming that either Jennifer paid for her parents' room or at least made the reservation."

"Probably the latter," Jim said.

"See if anyone saw Jennifer around there today. And have them find out if there's a clerk there named Jim. I'm going to assign some people to canvass this neighborhood. Surely someone saw a Firebird leave here when there was little other church traffic around. Is it a Trans Am?" he called after Jim, who was heading for the phone.

Veiled Threat
27

"No!"

"Well, in a way that's a break," Ellis said, barely above a whisper. "A black Firebird that's *not* a Trans Am might be easier to locate." He looked back to the group. "OK," he said, "there's not much need to hold everybody here. Anything else I should know before I check out the pastor's office and the back room?"

"I was just curious," Candy said, "if Mr. Hines remembers when I asked him to point Jennifer our way when she got off the phone. We switched rooms, and if we hadn't, like you say, one or two of us probably would have gone with her. We wouldn't have had any reason not to believe the message. I mean, not until we saw her parents here, both healthy."

"All that tells me," Ellis said, "is that either the person was working *very* close to the church, or there was a contingency plan to take care of any extra riders."

"Meaning?"

"I wouldn't want to speculate. I couldn't even tell you if whoever lured Jennifer away abducted her or not. And if they did, whether it was in the parking lot or down the street or at The Consulate or on the expressway. Who knows?"

"I'd like to answer the question the young lady posed," Hines said as Jim come back. "I remember promising to send her to you, but the pastor's office was empty when I checked again. I believe I told you I hadn't seen her when you asked about it later."

"But you told me she was in there," Jim said. "Remember—when I brought my tux in from the car?"

Hines thought for a moment. "Yes, I did. When I told you, I thought she was in there, and you said not to let you see her. That was just before I checked and found out she wasn't there."

"Did you try to find her?" Candy asked. "To tell her where the new dressing area was?"

"No. No, I didn't, and I don't remember why now. I think I figured if she wasn't in the pastor's office, she must have been out of there quite some time and had likely already caught up with the rest of the girls."

"Uh-huh," Candy said. "That's why the florist told me he'd seen you with Jim near the pastor's office, and I assumed Jim was with her in there after that."

"But she was already gone," Ellis said. "That helps pinpoint the time. Jim, didn't you notice that Jennifer's car wasn't in the lot when you arrived?"

"Yes, but I knew she had to have parked around the side or the front, because it was her car we were making our getaway in. In fact, I was a

28   Jennifer Grey Mysteries

little perturbed it wasn't right there handy so I could dump some stuff in it. But then I realized I didn't have the keys anyway, and I didn't want to see Jenn before the wedding."

Ellis Milton and Jim took a few minutes to debrief each other and to check out the pastor's office and the note Jennifer left on the blackboard in the original dressing room. Ellis called downtown and requested help canvassing the area. The response was not good.

"Wrong day to ask," he reported to Jim. "Lots of people off. Apparently, it's up to us."

"I gotta tell ya, it seems like a waste of time, El. Do we have to do it?"

"Oh, I think we definitely should, Jim. We have to have more than we've gotten so far. No doubt it was a phony call; at least, that's my guess. If it was just a mistake, the boys at The Consulate should be able to determine it quickly. But then Jennifer would have been back or called long before now. Let's ask for a couple of volunteers. There can't be that many homes around here, and we should do it now, while anything anyone might have seen would be fresh in their minds."

The phone rang. Ellis Milton picked it up. "Church office," he said, "Pastor Cass speaking."

"Pastor, this is Leo Stanton of the *Chicago Day*. Have the bride and groom left yet?"

"Is this for an article, sir?" Ellis asked.

"No, I'm Jennifer Grey's boss, and there's been some kind of a scam here. Could I speak to either Jennifer or Jim?"

"They're not available right now, Mr. Stanton," Ellis lied. "Can I help you in some way? What scam are you talking about?"

Jim's eyes lit up when he heard Stanton's name. He grabbed the phone. "Leo, this is Jim. What's up?"

"Well, well," Stanton said. "Are congratulations in order?"

"No, sir, I'm afraid not. Jennifer has been lured away or abducted somehow. Weren't you here?"

"No, that's what was so strange. I got a message to call my office just before I got to the church for the wedding. The reception on my car phone was fuzzy, so I called from a pay phone. The only person in the office on Sunday is the receptionist, who said there was an urgent, personal, confidential note waiting for me. When I arrived, the note was on my desk. It said that if I cared about my favorite columnist's health, I'd leave room for her column in tomorrow morning's paper. Jim, I didn't know what to make of it."

When Jim had filled in Ellis on the phone call and told him he didn't appreciate his deceiving Jennifer's boss, Ellis told him he was sure that a good, old-fashioned newspaperman like Leo Stanton had pulled a few similar tricks in his day and probably would get a kick out of knowing what had been pulled on him. "I'm going to ask him myself," Milton said. "Because if the only place we have someone actually contacting us in writing is at the *Chicago Day,* then that's where I'd like to set up shop."

Surprisingly, Ellis was right. In the midst of his confusion, turmoil, and fear over the life of his star columnist, Leo did remember a time when he was covering a tavern brawl where a man had been killed. The cops wouldn't let him in, so he went to a phone booth down the street, called the tavern, got the sergeant on the phone, and said, "This is Flanigan downtown at headquarters. What's goin' on over there?"

"And you got the whole story?" Ellis said, laughing.

"You bet!"

"Then we owed you one, didn't we?"

"I guess you did!"

Stanton agreed that Ellis could set up a command post at the *Day* after the neighborhood canvass. "Now all we need is to round up enough help to find out if anyone around here saw anything this afternoon," the detective told Jim.

Just before dismissing anyone who didn't want to help by asking basic questions door-to-door, Ellis asked if anyone had any more information about anything suspicious that might have happened at the church that day.

"There was one thing," Edwin Hines said. "The florist was convinced someone had been messing around near his truck. Said they stole his son's florist's smock. Don't know if that's significant or not."

Five

Double-A, Adolpho Alvarez, had largely ignored Jennifer during the first half of his repast. But when Maria attempted to pour Jennifer a cold drink, he flashed forward and batted the plastic, two-liter bottle against the wall. The cola fizzed and shot from the opening, splashing the carpet.

As if on cue, Luis Cardenas casually stood and went after a towel. He placed it over the puddle and set the bottle upright. He returned to his meal without finishing the cleanup.

Alvarez's eyes burned into Maria's face, but she acted as if nothing unusual had happened. Jennifer couldn't tell if Maria reacted calmly because such behavior was typical of Adolpho or because she knew that any resistance to his volatile temper would result in more violence.

"I'm thirsty," Jennifer had said, less calmly and evenly than she would have liked.

"She's thirsty," Alvarez said to Maria, ignoring Jennifer. "We haven't even talked yet. She's a guest in my house, and she asks for something to drink. She is a guest; she will be asked to cooperate, but we haven't even got that far, and she tells me she's thirsty. Tell her she will eat and drink from my table when I am ready, and I will not be ready until she agrees to cooperate."

"I have ears," Jennifer said. "You can talk to me."

She had clearly angered him now. Adolpho let his fork drop and, with his mouth full, he gripped the sides of the coffee table holding the food platter. Luis, Benito, and Maria leaned back, as if they knew what was coming.

The wide, hard man slid forward off the edge of his chair and squatted before the table. Still holding it only by the two sides of one end, he lifted it to his eyes. His biceps bulged, but there appeared to be no effort, no hesitation, no wavering. The table, heavy even if it hadn't been piled with food on a solid tray, was held flat, straight out.

Jennifer was impressed and pretended she wasn't.

"I could kill you with one bare hand," Adolpho said, slowly lowering the table. The others continued eating while he stared at Jennifer. "I don't need you," he added in his gravelly bass voice.

Veiled Threat

31

"Yes, you do," she said.

The other three looked up, startled. Jennifer had talked back to Adolpho after two outbursts and his show of strength. It was as if she was daring him to hurt her. "You need me for something," she said, "or you wouldn't have dared such a risky kidnapping."

He studied her and filled his mouth again. "When this is all over, you're gonna wind up gettin' yourself killed."

"Then why don't you let me eat anyway?"

Jennifer couldn't believe herself. For some reason, she was compelled to talk tough to this muscle man. She had hope. Hope that she would see Jim again. Hope that she would be married. Hope that she would go back to work and see her friends and co-workers. Hope that she would be able to go back to her church and her fellow believers. But somehow, sitting quietly and hoping and praying didn't seem to be enough.

If she riled the man to the point where he hurt her, then maybe she would be quiet. But she was no good to him dead; at least she was fairly certain of that. She still didn't know what he wanted. But if he planned to use her for more than just ransom bait, she would have to be alive and well and fed to do him any good. So she said so.

"Let her eat," Adolpho said, and Jennifer jumped. They were only three words, and they carried good news. But they hadn't been so fast or so distracting to hide the fact that A-A had slipped out of character for a moment. Those words, so quick off his tongue and vibrating with his trademark bass tones, had been completely devoid of a Mexican/Spanish accent. And Jennifer had not been able to mask her surprise.

Adolpho immediately started in again with a tirade of threats about what would happen to her if she chose not to cooperate after she had eaten. His accent was back, full and authentic as from one who had learned Spanish many years before learning English.

Then Jennifer, as the other three had done, simply ate, ignoring him. How quickly, she thought, one learned how to deal with A-A. And she was amazed—despite the disappointment in her gut, the fear in her heart, and the confusion in her mind—how delicious the food tasted.

It bore the trademark of authenticity. Succulent, mellow though lightly bitter, the intermingled flavors of corn and meal and flour and beans and rice and guacamole and beef and chicken and cheese and lettuce and tomato satisfied her hunger with the first ravenous bites.

But she couldn't force from her being the knowledge that her life was in danger. She was confused, dying for information. Not knowing what was going on had always been one of her deepest frustrations and probably the guiding force behind her becoming a journalist. Not only did she hate to be left out, she didn't even like being the second one to hear any news. She

32   Jennifer Grey Mysteries

had to know so she could be the one to tell. And right now, she knew nothing.

Just before Jennifer finished eating, Adolpho nodded to Benito and spoke softly to him. The younger man immediately put down his fork and went to another room. He emerged with a white business-sized envelope, which he was sliding into a 6- x 9-inch manila envelope. "Spell the name again for me, Maria, *por favor*," he said, pulling a black marker from a chest of drawers in the hall.

"S-T-A-N-T-O-N," she said, and he wrote in huge, block letters, adding, "URGENT."

Adolpho nodded to Diaz. "Come straight back," he said. "You'll need to take one of the eight-hour watches tonight."

Jennifer, who had casually been studying the room and whatever other parts of the apartment she could see, began to give up hope of an escape. If each of them were with her for eight-hour stretches, she wouldn't be getting far, even if she found a vulnerable window somewhere.

She didn't have to wonder which of the four would not be pulling guard duty, but she wished it were otherwise. She would have been willing to give up several hours of sleep—which she assumed would be fitful at best anyway—to talk with Adolpho Alvarez. Until now, he'd done most of the talking but hadn't said anything of substance.

Jennifer decided he was in his image-building mode. For all his braggadocio and showing off, she sensed a deep insecurity in the man. He felt the need to establish his power, his rank, his place, to beat his chest before not only Jennifer, but also his own underlings. In Jennifer's mind, Benito was quietly genuine. He was ruthless and violent without flaunting it. She almost feared him more. Because rather than trying to talk her out of her sarcasm, he'd just as soon blow her away.

Luis was much more quiet, fitting more Jennifer's stereotyped Mexican. She knew it was wrong to categorize any people, but with her limited contact with Mexicans and even Mexican-Americans—except at the office—she entertained the idea that the United States' immediate neighbors to the south were a quiet, easygoing type who took siestas and then slowly got back to industrious labor.

Already she had met four in one day who, except for Luis, shattered the mold. Adolpho was as boorish as any obnoxious American she had ever known. And he was far from easygoing. Maria, though she was obviously American born and bred, was just as obviously a full-blooded Mexican. But because of more than her lack of Spanish accent and manner of speech, she was the least like what Jennifer pictured a Mexican to be.

Veiled Threat

33

When Jennifer and the remaining three had left nothing but scraps on the platter, Adolpho stood, looking down on Luis. For some reason, Luis took that as a cue and quickly began rearranging the room. He waited for Maria to remove the food tray, then slid the coffee table out of the way. Then he dragged Adolpho's chair over in front of the couch.

Jennifer had a kneejerk reaction to help Maria with the cleanup and almost laughed aloud at herself. *Imagine*, she thought. *I'm kidnapped at gunpoint on my wedding day, see my new car destroyed, am brought who knows where for who knows what, and I still want to be a considerate guest!*

Instead, Jennifer sat where she had for the last hour or so and watched the silent theatre of Luis preparing the room for something and lazy Adolpho letting him do it, apparently to the do-nothing "Adonis's" specifications.

The air conditioner had quickly cooled Jennifer to the point that she was almost feeling a chill, but Luis was working up a sweat, rearranging the furniture. When Adolpho's chair was in place, he plopped down heavily, not because he was overweight—in fact, Jennifer thought he was in as solid good shape as anyone she had seen in a long time—but because of his big meal and maybe as a result of the fatigue showing in the redness around his eyes.

His chair was lined up with the center of the couch, and as Jennifer was sitting on the far end, to his left, she was able to avoid his squinting stare without having to turn too far away. "Excuse," Luis said, suddenly appearing in front of her. "You have my place."

She started to move, then stiffened. "Where would you like me?" she asked.

Luis motioned that she should move over to the middle of the couch, but that would have put her directly in front of Adolpho. She wasn't so sure she wanted to sit right next to Luis either. She slid down, past the middle to the other end.

Apparently, that was a breach of protocol. Both men looked shocked and angry and said in unison, "No, no!" and motioned her back to the middle. At first she didn't move, angered by the craziness of it all. But when Adolpho leaned forward and reached for her arm, she feigned to avoid him and slid the other way toward Luis.

Fortunately, Luis seemed as uncomfortable with her right next to him as she did. She didn't want to think what it would be like to sit almost touching Adolpho. She hoped she wouldn't have to find out.

The two men seemed to be waiting for Maria who was cleaning up the kitchen. Jennifer was tempted to impatiently demand to know what it was

34   Jennifer Grey Mysteries

all about, but she decided against it. Obviously, they were about to tell her what it was they wanted her to cooperate on, if she could only be patient. She figured she didn't have much choice anyway.

Maria returned with a smile as if she were a normal hostess glad to get back to her guest. If it hadn't been for Maria's earlier cold statement (behind as lovely a smile as she flashed now) that Jennifer would eat if she cooperated and wouldn't if she didn't, Jennifer might have wondered if Maria was in on this thing at all.

Maria sat next to Jennifer, who now had nowhere to look unless she wanted to encounter the high eyebrowed look of Luis; the expectant, cheery smile of Maria; or the bleary-eyed stare of Adolpho. She looked down.

As if to heighten the tension and prolong the agony, Adolpho said something to Maria in Spanish. She jumped up again and hurried to the kitchen, returning quickly with a huge glass mug, easily containing a full quart of icy beer. If Maria was offended by Adolpho's constant demands, she hid it well. She served it as if she was more than happy to do so. Jennifer decided Maria would have made a wonderful in-flight attendant.

From the corner of her eye, Jennifer watched as Adolpho took several long swallows of the beer. He set the mug on the floor next to his chair and leaned back so his seat was still on the front edge of the chair but his shoulders rested against the back. That position tucked his square chin into his chest. Still he stared directly at Jennifer.

With her knees almost touching his and each of her shoulders touching her other two guardians, Jennifer had never felt so vulnerable in her life. She smelled the alcohol on three breaths, but she guessed that none of the three was new to drinking and that none of them was to the point of inebriation yet.

Suddenly, as if now he was finally ready to begin his discourse, Adolpho slowly hunched himself up to where he was leaning forward toward Jennifer again. "I want you to look at me," he said.

She didn't.

"When I talk to you," he said louder, almost slurring, "I want you to look at me!"

Peripherally, she could see that even Luis and Maria were looking at him. She decided not to push him. She looked up with contempt and locked her eyes on his, trying with all her might to communicate with her look that she found him disgusting, despicable, beneath value.

She thought she might have gotten through. Under his baleful stare she sensed a wavering, a flicker of inconsistency, maybe even fear. For sure, he hated her; she could tell that. And she knew it was her calling to love her enemy. He was certainly that. She would deal with the theology later.

Veiled Threat   35

For now, she decided that communicating her true feelings to him through her eyes did not violate the broad truth that she should pray for him. She would pray for him later. Just now, she was praying for herself.

"I am the noble wolf," he said, but something was stuck in his throat. He said it as a pronouncement, but the obstruction in his voice made it sound like he had a bad connection. Jennifer almost laughed.

"You're the *what?*" she said derisively, pretending not to have completely heard him.

He cleared his throat, looking at her warily to decide whether she was mocking him or really wanting him to repeat it. He repeated it.

"I am the noble wolf."

He stared at her as if expecting some reaction. He should have been pleased with the first one. Jennifer had decided not to respond in any way. Let him wonder if she heard him this time. "And you," he said finally, clearly irritated by her lack of response, "will help the noble wolf and his Guest Workers Party."

Jennifer wanted to ask what she would be helping him accomplish, but she figured he would get to it.

"You will help us tell the United States about our plight. About our problems, the injustices, the needs of the Mexican people. You will help us tell your nation of the needy Mexican, the so-called illegal alien, and the charade your government called the Guest Worker program that allowed my people to come in and be taken advantage of. You will tell the story through your column that is sent around the country that if there are not changes in the way the United States treats Mexico and her people, violence will come to key people, the same way it will come to you."

Six

Candy Atkins, Pastor Howell Cass, custodian Edwin Hines, and Jim were the only volunteers for Detective Sergeant Ellis Milton's neighborhood canvassing detail. And after that, they would join Leo Stanton at the *Day*. Other police personnel would be assigned when they became available.

Having seen the florist's truck in the back parking lot, Ellis Milton erroneously assumed the petty theft of the smock happened there. He didn't know if it was related to Jennifer's disappearance, but if it was, he was guessing that Jennifer left by the back exit from the lot, rather than driving around the side of the church to the front.

"Pastor Cass and I will handle the street that runs behind the church at the far end of the parking lot," he told the four volunteers. "Then I'd like Jim and Candy to handle the houses across the street in front. Each of you start at either end, and when you meet in the middle, report what you've learned, if anything. Pastor, if either you or Candy come up with something interesting, tell your police partner, and we'll help you question the witness. Mr. Hines, if you'd stay here and wait for any phone calls, I'd appreciate it."

Ellis added to the canvassers, "I know time is important here, but I don't think we'll appear too authoritative or official in these getups. Let's change quickly and get to it."

After changing clothes, Jim and Candy talked briefly, then headed off on foot to either end of the block in front of the church. Jim found no one home at either of the first two houses, but the third had what appeared to be a family reunion going on in the backyard.

Jim flashed his badge and said, "Chicago PD," to the man at the outdoor grill.

"Hey, 'scuse me! We're not bein' too loud, are we? I mean, we got no music playin' or nothin' like that. You want me to tell 'em to keep the noise down—hey, I'll tell 'em. Someone squeal on us or something? Probably the old bat next door. Always a busybody, but, you know, if we're guilty, we're guilty. Did you think it sounded too noisy when you came around the side here?"

36

Veiled Threat

Jim assured him no one had called in any complaints about noise. "We're just checking out a missing person's report from the church across the way there."

"Oh, well, we never went there. We go to church, I mean, but not there, you know. Well, we go sorta sometimes, not all the time, not every Sunday. Certainly not twice every Sunday the way these people do. And Wednesday. Anyway, that's not my church. Never been there. Been visited by the pastor though. Nice guy. Wants us to come. We probably won't. You know anybody who goes to church that much?"

"I go to that church."

"Do you? Hey, that's nice, You go three times a week?"

Jim nodded.

"Boy oh boy, imagine a church good enough to draw people that often. Pretty good, huh?"

"Pretty good. Listen—"

"Hey, what happened over there today? We thought the wedding went pretty quick. My brother Fritz here was goin' on about how somebody had been jilted over there."

"You noticed the wedding went quickly, sir?"

"Oh, yeah, it seemed the last of the guests had just pulled in when we notice that they're all pullin' out. In fact, some of the latecomers were still gettin' there and the thing musta been already over! From the way the traffic came in, I woulda said there was a three o'clock wedding. But fifteen minutes later, it was a traffic jam. So, how you gonna find somebody missin' from that?"

"I don't know," Jim said. "Maybe I'm not. You hear or see anything strange or out of the ordinary around there today?"

"You mean, ah, when?"

"Before the wedding. Before most of the people arrived."

"Well, like what? I mean, we can't see much through the trees here, and we were all out here in the back."

"So nobody saw or heard anything unusual?"

"Don't think so. 'Cept Pudge, that's my son. Name's Paul, but we've always called him that. Tournament archer. You oughta see him shoot."

"He saw something?"

"Nope, heard something. The kid's a car buff, a whiz. He can hear a car that he can't see and can tell you what make, model, and year it is."

"He heard a car?"

"Heard screeching tires."

"And?"

"And what?"

"Did he see it?"

38   Jennifer Grey Mysteries

"No! He heard it! And he still knows what it was."

"Even the color?"

"Don't be silly."

"I could say the same to you, sir, to think anyone could know the year, make, and model of a car he can't see! The engines on several different makes and models are identical, made by the same suppliers even. How do you know he's right? Do you ever go check it out?"

"Never have to. We know he's right."

"Is he around?"

"Jes' a minute. Paul!"

A gangly, string-bean thirteen-year-old with taut muscles in his arms but nowhere else, jogged over to the two men. "Tell 'im, Pudge. Tell 'im how you can spot any car just by how it sounds."

"That's right, I can," the kid said, shaking hands. Jim was skeptical and didn't try to hide it.

"You heard a car screeching its tires between one-thirty and two o'clock over by the church?"

"Yes, sir, right out in front, just past those trees over there."

"Peeling rubber like it was taking off with a jackrabbit start, or slamming on the brakes?"

"Braking. Like it was going kinda fast, then hit the hooks, you know?"

Jim nodded.

"And then it drove off?"

"No, I heard a door open and shut, and then it drove off."

"So someone got out?"

"Or in."

"True enough. And you know what kinda car it was?"

"Nah."

"What?" his father demanded. "You always told us what kinda cars they are! What'sa matter?"

"Aw, Dad, all I can tell from the sound is the size of the engine and whether it's a four-barrel or not, that's all. And I can tell if it's automatic or stick, that kinda stuff. I always guess a kind of car 'cause I know you get a kick out of it. Half the time I'm right because there are only so many cars that have that kind of equipment."

His father shook his head, embarrassed and clearly irritated. "Well, don't be makin' up something for this guy, 'cause he's a cop. Give 'im the straight dope, and don't be givin' me tall stories anymore either. OK?"

Paul shrugged. "This was a big, four-barrel automatic. Could have been a Corvette or Camaro—though they don't make too many of the loaded Camaros like they used to."

Veiled Threat   39

"If it could have been a Camaro, it could have been a Firebird, right, son?" Jim asked. Paul nodded. "Sure. More likely. Probably a Trans Am."

"But it wouldn't have to be."

"No. I guess you *could* soup up a Firebird without havin' it be a Trans Am, but probably only a woman would do that, and no woman would have been driving like that today."

"If the driver was showing off, you mean?"

"Yeah, and that's what it sounded like."

"But if the driver really almost hit something or someone?"

"Then it could have been anybody."

"One more thing, Paul. What color did it sound like?"

"Hah!" Paul said, kicking the ground. "Cute."

When Jim went back around to the front of the house, Candy was coming up the sidewalk. "This is it?" she asked. "You've only been to three houses?"

"Yeah, sorry. How many did you hit?"

"Eight. I kept thinking I was going to run into you."

"This was the only place with anybody home. Didn't get much, except I think Jennifer must have come out of the lot the front way, hit the brakes, a door opened and shut, and took off again. How'd you make out?"

"About the same. My people were home, but only one would let me in. A couple said they noticed the wedding was pretty short. Three said they heard a near accident at about one-thirty or a little before. Only the little old lady in this brick house here next door invited me in. I think she saw Jennifer, Jim, and I thought you'd better handle the interview."

Jim walked toward the house. "What makes you think she saw her?" he asked.

"She's a widow. Four years. Gets her work done early in the morning, and I mean *early*. Like at sunup even in the summer. That gives her the rest of the day to watch out the window, she says. She's watching us now. She reads her paper on a little TV tray next to the window. Takes her phone calls there. Eats her meals there. Doesn't own a TV. Wouldn't know what to do with it. Sunday's her favorite day. Lots of people to watch twice a day, and even more today because of the wedding."

"I'm Jewish," the little, white-haired woman explained as she let Jim and Candy inside. "I go to synagogue on Saturday and have Sundays all to myself. I was getting myself a late lunch in the kitchen, or I would have seen where the little black car came from. It makes me so mad. I knew you were coming to ask me. I saw you come out of the church. I knew something was wrong because the wedding was so short, but I didn't know

40   Jennifer Grey Mysteries

if the accident—or the almost accident, I should say—had anything to do with that or not. I feel so bad that I didn't see where that car came from."

"That's all right, Mrs.—"

"Freidrichsen," she said.

"Yes, that's all right," Jim said. "Could you just tell us what you did see?"

"Well, I watched all the people come to church this morning. They have some kind of religious training classes early, I believe, and many people come for that. But even more come later for the worship ceremony or pageant—I've never attended, of course—and though some of those who arrived early leave when the others get there, most don't, so the biggest total crowd is for the later meeting. Then I knew there was a wedding because I saw more than the usual number of cars stay behind at the end. And then I saw the florist's truck. Not enough cars arrived before one o'clock for it to be a one o'clock wedding, and no one has a wedding on the half hour, do they? So I watched the girls arrive and one or two of the men, carrying their fancy clothes. And I dashed to the kitchen some time after one-fifteen or so and made myself a tuna sandwich, which I love. Do you?"

Jim wanted to shrug, but he nodded, as did Candy, smiling.

"And as I sat back down by the window with my tea, I heard the roar of the engine in the black car, a little car, very fast."

"Tiny?" Candy prompted.

"No, not like a tiny foreign car. More like a teenager's fast car, only the driver was a woman. Not too young. Not too old. Long, brown hair."

"The car was going fast, but you could tell it was a woman driving?" Jim asked.

"Well, it was on my side of the street, and when she almost hit the florist, she stopped suddenly and sat there for a moment."

"She almost hit the florist?"

"Yes! What he was doing in the street, I don't know, because his truck was parked on the church side, and he certainly didn't need to get over here for anything. It was as if he jumped out in front of her on purpose!"

"How do you know it was the florist?"

"Well, florist's helper then."

"No, I'm not saying it wasn't the florist, ma'am, I was just asking—"

"I know it wasn't the florist because the truck had an Italian name on it, and this boy was not Italian."

"What was he?"

"Cuban maybe? Puerto Rican? South American? Something like that."

"Can you describe him?"

"Maybe twenty. Not too tall. Black hair, moustache."

Veiled Threat 41

"And you thought he worked with the florist because—"

"Because he had a florist's coat on, a green smock, the kind they wear."

"Uh-huh, and what happened?"

"Well, I heard the engine, so the black car was not going fast until it got near my house, I guess. Like it was going normally and then started going fast, you know?"

"Or as if it were coming out of the church parking lot from the rear?"

"I suppose, but I didn't see it in time. I'm sorry."

"That's all right. What else?"

"Well, just before she got up to the florist's truck, this young Latino man seemed to jump in front of her car, waving his arms. She slammed on the brakes and swerved onto my parkway there. You can see the tracks."

"And she missed him."

"Yes. She sat there for a moment and seemed to be putting the car in gear again or getting ready to go somehow, and the young man walked in front of the car with his hand up. He opened the door on this side and got in. They talked for a minute, and then she pulled away. That's all I know."

Seven

Adolpho Alvarez, the self-proclaimed noble wolf, was on a roll. Full of Mexican delights he had tastily prepared himself and loosened by a full quart of ice-cold beer (after having downed a few normal-sized ones during his late lunch), he sat before Luis Cardenas to his left, the abducted Jennifer Grey in the center, and his wife—if Jennifer could believe that— on his right.

And he was carrying on. Despite all the food and beer that made him groggy and short of breath, Double-A was not a fat man. Big, yes. Stocky. Not too tall. Musclebound, his sleeveless shirt displaying bulging biceps and a bulky, taut neck, he was engaged in a lengthy tirade about injustice.

Jennifer felt weak, despite having eaten heartily from her kidnappers' table. The air conditioner had long since cooled her past the point of comfort, yet it continued to labor and drone on. No one else seemed the least bit bothered by it, and she guessed that was because they had suffered so long in their native country without such a convenience.

"My country is made up of Spanish people," Alvarez was slurring, "Indians—about a third, and the rest a mixture. Mestizos. Luis here, he is Indian. Maria is Spanish, born in America of full-blooded Spanish Mexicans. Benito and me, we are Mestizo."

Jennifer wanted to ask where Adolpho had met Maria, but she was not in a reporting situation. The way the lecture was going, she figured he might get to that anyway. Sometimes, when Adolpho slipped into Spanish, Maria would quietly turn to Jennifer and translate.

"The most powerful organization in Mexico, before the noble wolf formed the Guest Workers Party, was the Partido Revolucionario Institucional."

"Institutional Revolutionary Party," Maria whispered. "Or the authentic party of the revolution."

"They have a rival in PAN," Adolpho said. "The Partido Acion Nacional."

"National Action Party," Maria said.

"Both partidos think that because Mexico has a so-called stable government—and I suppose it is more stable than anything else south of

42

the United States—that it will soon become a major industrial power with all its oil reserves."

He paused for a reaction. Jennifer felt like screaming. Anything for a change. She was cramped, crowded, stifled. The three all had beer breath. "And you disagree, no doubt," she said.

That she said anything caused Adolpho to flinch, and he sneered as he fought to decide whether she had been disrespectful. He decided she had not, mostly because she had asked him a question he wanted to answer.

"Of course, I disagree," he said. "Mexico will never be prosperous until they make me at least governor of the federal district."

"I'm sorry," Jennifer said, wishing as she said it that she hadn't seemed subservient. "But I don't know enough about the inner workings of the government of your country to understand what that means."

She had irritated him. Adolpho was offended that she didn't know more about something so close to him. "The federal district!" he shouted. "I don't wanna be in charge of any of the thirty-one states. I want to be appointed governor of the federal district."

"And who makes that appointment?"

"The president."

"And he selected someone else?"

"Of course! He would not even speak to me, see me, return my calls, answer my letters. I had a petition from many hundreds of people who wanted to see me in some station of national authority."

"Did you have the credentials?"

"The credentials? I am the noble wolf! I am the one who saw through the crazy scheme our president and your president worked out at Camp David a few years ago. One hundred thousand guest workers were to be allowed to visit the United States for two years, and the number of visas for legal immigration to your country was supposed to be increased to forty thousand."

"And that didn't happen?" Jennifer asked.

"Yes! It happened! It was a success! So why has nothing come of it? Most of the guest workers, myself included, have been deported."

"Because the plan didn't work?"

"Because it *did* work! Americans are threatened by foreign workers who know how to work hard, who show that Americans are lazy and cannot keep up. The program worked all too well, and the American unions couldn't take it."

"You met Maria while you were here on the program?"

He nodded slowly. "I was not here the whole two years."

44   Jennifer Grey Mysteries

He had said it flatly, as if it was incidental. Jennifer picked up on it immediately. "Of course, you weren't," she said. "You were a troublemaker, a rabble-rouser, a malcontent. Am I right?"

At first he looked offended, then he smiled wryly as if he liked her spunk. "I was not thrown out, if that's what you think."

"Then where did you go?"

"Back to Mexico."

"For what?"

"To try to join the big labor union. The *Union Confederacion de Trabajadores de Mexico*. More than two million Mexicans belong to this union and still have to work forty-eight hours a week. Millions of Mexicans still can't read or write."

"And so you tried to improve things by working in the union?"

"I was not allowed in the union either. I had brought my American wife with me, and even though she is Mexican and looks Mexican, she did not sound Mexican, and we were found out. I had trouble finding any work at all, even though I am the noble wolf and had the best interests of my people at heart."

"But there isn't anything wrong with an American living in Mexico, is there?"

"Not officially, no. But when so many Mexicans are kept out of the U.S., they do not like Americans going down there either. I was not welcome among the very people I was trying to help."

"And so you—?"

"Came back here. I still had my visa, which had been canceled, but which I was able to duplicate."

"It must not have taken the authorities long to find out you were here illegally."

"Not long."

There was a knock at the door. One knock, then a pause, then another single knock. Maria ran to open it. "Benito?" she asked.

"Si."

Benito came in smiling. "Mission accomplished?" Maria asked, as she had when he and Luis had brought Jennifer up the stairs. He nodded.

"Anyone see you?" Adolpho asked.

"No. This was a perfect day for it because so few people were at the newspaper office. I waited until the receptionist was on the phone, then I left the envelope right in front of her where she could see it when she turned around."

"Do you think he got the envelope?" Adolpho said.

Benito nodded.

Veiled Threat 45

"And you weren't seen?"

He shook his head.

"Good job. Have a beer and sit down."

"Are you going to get to your point?" Jennifer asked.

"Sure," Adolpho said. "But first you're gonna hear how we kept your column open in tomorrow's paper."

"Impossible."

"No. We called Stanton on his car phone, Maria using her best English and yet faking a bad connection well enough to keep him from realizing it was a phony call. He was to head back to his office for an emergency. When he got there, no emergency, but a message from us."

"Which said?"

"Trust me," Adolpho said. "He will keep a spot open for you."

"So you needlessly scared him."

"Needlessly? You don't seem to realize how important your column is to us."

"This reminds me of those radio and TV station takeovers in the nineteen sixties."

"So we're behind the times? It seems to me we are on the forefront of revolutionary activity."

"What do you want from me?"

"It seems to me you could guess."

"I can't," Jennifer said. "And don't expect me to try."

"You will be writing your column for the next several days. Or weeks. As long as it takes for us to accomplish our goals."

"Which are?"

"Sympathy for our cause."

"You've been going on and on, and I still don't know what your cause is."

"That is because you are a true American. You could never see, never understand. That is why you must just listen and let me tell you what to write."

"You think anybody will believe that I wrote it?"

"Sure. You are going to phrase it in such a way as to give it, ah, credibility. It will be coming from you and not from me."

"And will you let me tell the truth? Will you let me tell that I have been kidnapped and forced to write?"

"Of course! Everyone should know that by now anyway. It will show the seriousness of our mission and our message."

"Which I still don't understand."

"You will when I tell you what to write."

"And where will I write?"

46   **Jennifer Grey Mysteries**

Adolpho beamed. "Come with me," he said. He stood and stretched and groaned loudly. Jennifer followed him down the hall to a big bedroom next to a bathroom. Her bags had been opened and ransacked, her clothes hung in the closet.

As she stepped into the room she realized that the other three captors had followed her. Now they and Adolpho stood with her, eager to see her reaction, as if she had just rented an apartment and they wanted to know how she liked it. She was expressionless. There was no window. Just a big bed, a big closet, and in the corner with a quaint lamp, a small, wood desk.

"Bring in the surprise," Adolpho said.

Luis moved to another room and returned, lugging a huge box that had not been opened. It was marked "fragile," and there were myriad instructions on how to store it, how to open it, how to remove the contents, and why to save the box. It took all three men to pull the heavy, gleaming typewriter from the box.

Had Jennifer not been used to video display terminals and state-of-the-art computer typesetting technology, she might have been impressed.

"Freshly bought, huh?" was all she could muster.

"Freshly stolen," Adolpho said with a grin. "In the name of the Guest Workers Party of the United Mexican States, we have appropriated the equipment. You will type your column on this, and we will deliver it to a different place each day. Then we will call your editor and tell him where to find it."

"You know, the other papers around the country who carry my column have been told that I will not be writing it for three weeks."

"They'll make room for this story, señora," Adolpho said. "We have done our homework. We know how rich and famous and important you are. When you are reported missing and still unmarried, it will be big news. And when the papers find out you are writing your column in exile, they will run it. Don't think they won't."

"You have been doing your homework, haven't you?"

"For this payoff, honey?" Benito said. "You better believe it. We been studyin' you and your boss and your boyfriend and your pastor and your church and everything for weeks. It'll be worth it."

"What he means," Adolpho said, glaring at Benito, "is that what we are seeking for our people is a big, important concession from your government, and so everything we do for the working man of Mexico is worth any sacrifice."

"Did you study enough to know when my deadlines are?"

"Your deadlines are when we say they are. They will hold the presses for you."

"But not forever. Especially if you have to deliver what I write."

Veiled Threat

47

"Then let's get started."

"Do you have paper?"

Adolpho swore. Maria told him they had some yellow legal pads. "That will have to do," he said. "Can you type on those?"

"I can type on anything," Jennifer said. "But the question is: Will I?"

Adolpho had had enough. He was troubled, frustrated, irritated at his insubordinate prisoner. He turned to face her, and the other three immediately left the room, sensing his anger and not wanting to be there if he erupted.

"Let me tell you something, lady," he said slowly through clenched teeth, leaning close to Jennifer so she could smell him and his breath. "Many writers would give anything for the opportunity you have. You were selected for a reason because you are good, and your column is read by millions all over the world. You think we would have chosen just anyone? You should feel lucky. This will make you even bigger. What you write and the reaction you get could change history. You will be affecting U.S.-Mexican relations maybe for the rest of our lives. And you will be gaining for the poor Mexican working man a dignity and a life-style he deserves."

"Touching," Jennifer said.

Adolpho put both hands on Jennifer's shoulders, but hardly in a compassionate way. He was trembling with rage, and she was scared. "If you make light of me or my mission, or if you disobey me, I will kill you."

"And then what good will I be to you?"

"You will be, at least, an example to whomever follows you to my cause. But I will not kill you until you have served me."

"And if I refuse to serve you?"

"Then I will start with your man, Jim Purcell. I know where he lives. I know his phone number. I know his car. I know his schedule, his habits—everything. He would be easy. Almost as easy as your parents, George and Lillian Knight of Rockford. And your older brother. And your younger sister. And their families. You will do what I say, Mrs. Grey, because I know everything about you and them. I know how to get to you. You may not fear for your own life. I even know that because I have studied your religion. But you care for the lives of others, especially your loved ones. You wouldn't want to see them hurt or killed at the hands of the Guest Workers Party, would you?"

Jennifer shook her head, knowing that she would do almost anything he asked. She tried to pull back from his grip, but his fingers tightened. Maria entered with the paper, and Adolpho dropped his hands, backing away.

48 Jennifer Grey Mysteries

Maria plugged in the typewriter and turned it on. Jennifer fed the paper in and tapped a few keys to see what it looked like. It looked like nothing. Adolpho, leaning over her shoulder, swore again.

"There's no ribbon," Jennifer said. She looked at the box. "Ribbon and correcting tape not included," it read.

"Do you need it?"

"Correcting tape, no. Ribbon, absolutely."

"We gotta go get some. Luis!"

Eight

Jim and Candy jogged behind the church and into the parking lot where the pastor and Ellis Milton were strolling back. Ellis reported that no one on their tour had seen or heard anything suspicious, except that the wedding or meeting or whatever it was supposed to be was certainly short.

Jim told him what Candy and he had discovered. "Let me get this down and draw some conclusions," the detective said. "Then let's get down to the *Day* and we'd better take separate cars. I can't guarantee how long we'll be there or when any of you might want to get home and get some sleep."

While Ellis was making notes on the white-hot trunk of his car, Ed Hines emerged from the church with the news that the police investigators at The Consulate Hotel were satisfied that no one from there had suffered any sort of illness and also that there was no evidence that any calls had been placed from The Consulate to the church.

"That means that this man who jumped in front of Jennifer's car either placed the call that threw Leo Stanton off the track or tipped someone else off to make the call, and he probably called Jennifer at the church to flush her out. I can't imagine he's working alone, but on this part of it, he apparently was. We need to see if there's a phone booth close by, close enough for him to have placed the call and then still have gotten back to the church in time to intercept Jennifer."

Ellis instructed the others to drive on downtown to the *Day* offices and to let Leo Stanton know that he and Jim would be along. Ellis drove slowly down the street in front of the church. About two hundred feet from the front of the building was a gas station on the church's side of the street at the corner. Out in front was a phone booth.

"Help you?" the attendant asked.

"Yeah, maybe," Ellis said, showing his badge and identifying himself. "Looking for a male Latino, early to mid-twenties, black hair, moustache, short and stocky but not too fat. Might have made a phone call here sometime after one o'clock this afternoon."

"Ah, I was workin' on a car between one and two. Lemme ask Rodney. Hey, Rod!" The attendant explained the question to the young pump man.

49

50 Jennifer Grey Mysteries

"Yeah, I saw him. Kinda strange. Looked like he was carryin' a piece too. Had it stuck in his belt and was tryin' to hide it with his black shirt. He was wearin' all black. Went to the phone, made a call, then watched up the street for about a minute and started jogging that way. Yeah, I remember him. He didn't say nothin' or do anything around here. Just made the call and ran up that way, that's all."

"How did you happen to notice him?"

"Well, I have this little old man who always pulls up to the self-service pumps and then gets someone to help him anyway. I was out there pumpin' his gas for him when this guy got off the bus, wandered up the street a ways, came back, made his phone call, then hurried up the street. I didn't see him again after that."

As both attendants got back to work, Ellis told Jim he was going to try something. "Put a watch on me," he said.

Jim looked at his watch and said, "Go."

Ellis stood at the bus stop and walked halfway down the street toward the church. "I can see the back and front at the same time," he said. "Can you?"

"Sure can," Jim said. "And took you less than a minute, moving casually."

"So, I go this way to determine that Jennifer's car is in the lot—that tells me she's in the church. I've already got my story concocted. If anyone else answers the phone, I tell them to tell her it's you. Makes sense. Unless you're already there, which I can also tell from just up the street. Then, when she comes to the phone, I tell her what? That I'm from The Consulate and that her father has had a heart attack. No time for anything else, she has to come. Now, put a watch on me again. I'm going to jog up from the phone booth."

Ellis trotted from the phone booth to halfway down the street where he could watch the parking lot. "See?" he said, huffing as he moved toward the church. "From here I can see her come out to her car. I can dash up to the florist's truck and grab a smock—for who knows what reason? Maybe so that if she comes this way I can make her think I'm a florist. If she goes out the back, I can still run that way and head her off. But she goes this way, so I've got the smock, I jump in front of the car and make her stop to keep from hitting me. Gutsy. Then somehow I get in the car with her. If she's got anyone with her, I can do away with them or scare them or something."

"Probably do away with them if he's got a gun the way the gas station guy thought," Jim said. "Otherwise, they could identify him. Listen, would it do any good to see if the bus driver knows where he picked him up?"

Veiled Threat

51

"Might, but the odds are bad. He probably came a great distance with transfers, maybe part of the way by cab. It'd be awfully hard trying to trace him very far back."

"The only thing that doesn't add up so far," Jim said as they went inside the church, "is his risking the time to get the smock. Think that was planned or just a spur-of-the-moment thing?"

"Had to be spur of the moment, because he couldn't have known for sure the florist would be here or exactly where he would park either."

"But would he really have had time?"

"I don't know. What'd you get on me from the phone call to where the florist's van was?"

"Less than thirty seconds."

"And what did Jennifer do in here? Let's run through it. She put the phone down here, then moved into the first dressing room and wrote the note after looking around for anyone close by. Maybe she was slipping on her shoes and grabbing her keys at the same time. Then she headed out the back to the car. How much time?"

"Almost a minute. He had plenty of time. Let's get downtown."

In the car, Jim asked, "What've we got? What do we know?"

"Precious little," Ellis said.

"That's what I was thinking."

"You worried?"

"Wouldn't you be? What kind of a question is that?"

"Well, we know for sure she was abducted. She didn't leave on her own. We know her father is all right, so a bogus message was used to lure her away. We know someone wants to use her column for some reason."

"Ransom?" Jim asked.

"Likely. Maybe something bigger. We'll learn more every time we hear from the abductors. The Latino appearance of the one may be a clue. But it may mean nothing. We can put our international terrorist specialists on it and see if any of the groups have been operating in or around Chicago or the Midwest. But he could just be a member of a bigger group."

"You don't think he could be working alone?"

"Unlikely. This thing is a little polished, even in its danger. I mean, kidnapping someone in broad daylight the way he did it is about as risky as I've heard in a long time. Usually, it's either your amateurs or your Mafia types that get away with that. It's either a spectacular success or a spectacular failure."

"I hope this is a failure," Jim said.

"So far it's a big success, and it's going to take all we've got to crack it. I hope you know that."

"I do. That's why I'm worried."

52 Jennifer Grey Mysteries

"You're a religious guy, Jim. Thought you weren't supposed to worry."

"I'm a human being."

"But isn't worry a lack of faith in God?"

"Oh, I don't think so. I have faith that God is doing His perfect will. But I worry that that perfect will might contain something I'm not ready for yet. Maybe I'm about to learn a tough lesson I didn't even know I needed."

"You mean like if God would let something happen to Jennifer, you would think He was trying to tell you something?"

"It's possible."

"And that's the kind of a God you believe in?"

"Hey, Ellis, this is a pretty tough time to make me try to defend God, you know what I mean?"

"Yeah, I guess. Sorry. It's just that you're a religious kind of a person, and yet something like this happens to you, just like anybody else."

"It's not as if God did it, though, Ellis. He may have allowed it, but I can't blame Him for it."

"But you'll pray it works out, and what if it doesn't?"

"Then I'll need God to give me the strength to bear it. Because I sure don't have that kind of strength in myself."

"But you're a religious—"

"How many times have you said that now, El? I'm not religious. If I were religious, maybe I would have some sort of strength in myself. A true believer knows he has no resources and trusts in a Person. That Person gives the strength that the believer would otherwise not have."

"And that Person is God?"

"Yes, in the form of His Son."

"Jesus Christ."

"Right."

"That simple."

"Not so simple, as you can see from the predicament I'm in now."

"Well, Jimbo, at least you're honest. I've seen religious types, I mean—sorry—uh, believers who pretend that nothing bothers them. They smile through the disappearance of a child or the murder of a spouse or the loss of their home."

"They may have peace from God."

"Yeah, but like you say, they're human beings. Doesn't God allow people to be weak, to grieve, to be honest, to face themselves and their losses?"

"I think He does."

"Well, so do I. And these people who put on this phony relig—er, 'churchy' facade as if nothing at all can get 'em down, they wind up on a funny farm somewhere, because eventually it all catches up with them.

Veiled Threat

53

You know, the first time I encountered that, it was an old man whose wife of fifty-some years had been robbed and beaten to death right in front of him. Well, he was so calm and cool and collected that I was intrigued by whatever it was he had that I didn't have. He said he was a Christian. Well, who isn't a Christian, you know? But he had a different brand, a real church-goin', Bible-readin', life-livin' style that really got to me. He said he was frustrated and upset that he hadn't been able to help his dear wife, but that he knew she was with Jesus, which proved that the whole thing was meant to be."

"I can see how that would be confusing, Ellis. I really can. I'm afraid I wouldn't be that way. I'm afraid that in spite of my faith, I would be asking God a lot of questions. And I think my healing period would be lengthy. I don't even want to think about it."

"Like I say, Jim, at least you're honest. Realistic. Maybe that way, if anything bad happens to Jennifer, you won't wind up killin' yourself the way the old man did."

"He did, really?"

"Yup. He did. I always thought that if he had just let his faith in God be his comfort instead of his excuse, he might have been OK."

"I'll buy that. But you know, Ellis, the thing I always have to keep coming back to is that no matter what happens, there's a God out there who's personally interested in us. I mean, what kind of a God would He be if He wasn't? A God reserved just for churches smacks too much of institutionalized religion."

"Yeah," Ellis said. "The type that preys upon people and takes advantage of them."

"Sometimes it does, yes. But God Himself, the true God, doesn't. I believe that when someone honestly seeks God and asks Him to reveal Himself, He has to respond to that. I mean, if a person prayed, 'God, if You're out there, let me know,' God would have to somehow let him know."

Ellis was silent, staring straight ahead as he neared the *Chicago Day*. "I've been a Christian almost all my life, El," Jim continued, "and I have to say, that's the one thing that I've never gotten over. That God cares about people individually, you and me. The God who created the universe, if you can believe it, actually loves me. Loves you. Isn't that incredible?"

"Like you said, Jim. If you can believe it."

"I want to believe it, El."

"That's probably why you do."

"That's not the only reason. I asked God to reveal Himself to me."

"And did He?"

54   Jennifer Grey Mysteries

"Yes. It wasn't long after I asked Him to do that that I ran into people of faith, people who believed. I saw God in them. I was attracted to God through them."

Ellis Milton pulled into the parking lot behind the *Day* building. "If you're a praying man," he said in a conversation-ending tone, "you'd better start praying about this case. It's gonna be a tough one."

"Don't think I haven't started."

Pastor Cass and Ed Hines had already decided they would only be in the way and had left the newspaper office a few minutes before. "Nice couple of guys," Leo Stanton said, dragging a couple of extra chairs into his spacious office. Candy Atkins greeted Ellis and Jim, then resumed her posture with her head in her hands. She had been crying.

"You all right, Candy?" Jim asked.

"I'm not sure. This really has me spooked. I have this dread fear for Jennifer. And I feel helpless; there's nothing I can do for her."

"I feel the same way," Jim said, briefly resting his hand on her shoulder.

"Hey, let's not be so glum," Leo said, his tall, rangy, Ivy League look suffering only slightly from fatigue. "You know we're gonna hear from these guys, and they're gonna tell us what they want."

"And if it's not too unreasonable, we'll try to smoke 'em out," Ellis said. "That's all we can do."

"What's unreasonable?" Candy asked. "Seems to me if they ask for a million dollars, you still try something."

"Money is no problem," Ellis said. "You can always fake something with money. It's when they want to talk to the President or get a plane to somewhere or get some political prisoners released. That's when your hostage's life is in danger. They want to start proving they mean business. Remember the Arab-Israeli thing at the 1972 Olympics?"

Ellis filled in Leo and Candy on all the developments up to that point. Then Leo asked, "Now what?"

"Now we sit and wait," Ellis said. "The next move is theirs. We don't know where they are, who they are, how many there are, what they want—besides a column by Jennifer—or when they want it. I need to call downtown and get some telephone guys over here to try to trace any calls. Meanwhile, tell me what you've done, if anything."

"I put a note about Jennifer's disappearance out over the wire and gave strict instructions not to call here for details. I included the fact that she was abducted from her church on her wedding day and that we would send new information as it became available. I did notify the papers who carry her column that one would be forthcoming, but I made no promises when or what length, or whether it would be publishable. I didn't get any phone

Veiled Threat

calls which I appreciated—but our teletype machine lit up with requests from all kinds of papers, ones that never carried her column before, to be put onto the service immediately. They're also demanding to know if she's being forced by someone to write a column. Many are going to press within a couple of hours, and some are holding press runs already. They're onto the story, and I'm going to have to tell them the whole truth soon."

"Oh, do it right away," Ellis said. "The more people who print the abduction story, the more who will read it. I want the whole country to be looking for Jennifer. Also, their show of support could scare the kidnappers. Letters to the editor, offers of money to start a ransom fund. That'll make 'em nervous."

"I hope it doesn't make them do something rash," Jim said.

"Jim," Ellis responded, "they already have."

Nine

It had become quickly apparent to Jennifer that though Alvarez was the leader, Diaz the sergeant at arms, and Cardenas a follower, Maria Ruiz was the brains of the Guest Workers Party. Double-A had assigned Cardenas to "rip off some typewriter ribbons somewhere," but it was Adolpho's wife, Maria, who kept Luis from otherwise wasting his time.

When Alvarez was somewhere else, Maria tore the side of the typewriter box and slipped it to Luis. She told him in Spanish, "You must find only this kind, no other. Remember, nothing else will fit."

"Where should I look?"

"Not in a department store. It must be a specialty store or a stationery store. You might have to buy it to be safe. Otherwise, you will have to bring many kinds if you don't have time to read the serial numbers. Better to get help and ask for the right kind."

Cardenas found that humorous, but when he got out searching for the right ribbons, he soon realized he would indeed have to buy them rather than shoplift them. They were hidden away and complicated to figure out. And they were expensive. He embedded the name and location of the store in his memory so he could make up for the purchase some other time. He was a couple of hours getting back, and Adolpho was angry. He stomped around the apartment, breathing heavily.

"Let's get on with it," he said. Jennifer put the ribbon into the typewriter and asked Adolpho how he wanted to work.

"What do you mean, 'how do I want to work?'" he asked. "I'm gonna tell you what to write, that's what."

"And all these people are going to be in here watching me type, is that it?"

Luis and Benito sat on the bed; Maria was on the floor, her back to the wall.

"Yeah," A-A said. "You got a problem with that or what?"

"I guess not," Jennifer said, realizing that her wishes made little difference. "But I'll tell you this, unless you write like I do, this column is going to sound phonier than a Mexican leader who fakes his native accent."

Veiled Threat   57

Adolpho glared at her. He was silent for a moment, as if wondering how to save face in front of his people. "So," he said finally, "how do *you* propose that we work?"

"You let me interview you, and then you let me write the column my own way. If you expect anyone to believe you or think your cause has any credibility, you have to let me lend it. Otherwise, I'm just a kidnapped typist, banging out what you force me to bang out on your stolen typewriter."

"I'll think about it," Alvarez said. "What if you write what I don't like?"

"Then you change it if you must. I'll guarantee one thing: Unless you force me to write something I disagree with, you won't like what I write. But you will get notoriety and attention. I have to hand it to you on that score; if my usual papers print me, you'll have quite an audience."

"OK," Alvarez decided. "You interview me."

Maria brought paper and a pen, and Jennifer began her questioning. "Tell me about yourself. Who are you? Where did you come from? And what do you want?"

"Adolpho Alvarez is the noble wolf. I was born in Monterey, Mexico, of poor parents, thirty-nine years ago. My father was a farmer and my mother a seamstress, and they both died at a very young age, younger than I am now. The work, the land, the poverty was too much for them. I worked in factories in the city when I was fourteen and began to learn the ways of management against labor. By the time I was twenty, I was a powerful union leader in my country. Though I never held an elected position, except in the local unions, many workers looked to me as their leader."

Alvarez quit talking as if satisfied with the portrait he had painted of himself. "How did you build yourself up, physically I mean?" Jennifer asked.

He beamed. "I was always a hard worker, and when the work began to develop the muscles, I decided to help the development along. I worked with weights, but we had to make them ourselves. We had no money for store-bought weights. We used pipes and buckets and cement, and we read books and magazines about how to build the muscles and the body. Good job, eh?"

Jennifer didn't respond. "Is that all you want to tell me?"

"I will tell you anything you ask."

"What do you want?"

"Justice for the people."

"What people?"

"*All* people."

"Even people like me?"

58   Jennifer Grey Mysteries

"Of course!"

"Was it 'just' to kidnap me?"

"On the day of your wedding, you mean?" he asked, eyes twinkling.

"At all, forget what day you did it on."

Alvarez walked over to the door and stretched to fill the frame with his arms. He pushed up and the wood creaked. He groaned loudly, as if tired. "Sometimes," he said carefully, seeming almost to stand straighter as he delivered the line, "a small injustice is worth the greater justice that might come from it."

Jennifer sat back and sighed after she had noted the quote. "That was almost poetic," she said. "The only potentially valid thing I've heard you say today."

He dropped his arms and stepped toward her menacingly. "Oh, quit trying to scare me," she said. "I'm getting a little weary of your posturing. You've got these people scared to death of you so they'll do anything you say. And I believe harm might come to my loved ones if I don't do what you say, so stop with the theatrics. You wouldn't hurt them yourself, because you're a coward. You'd send Benito with his weapon or Luis with his blind obedience. You might hurt me because you know I'm no match for you. If you want me to use my column, waste my space, use the readers and the editors who trust me to further your cause, you're going to have to get to it. What is it you want?"

"Justice!"

"You said that. What do you *mean?* Are you telling me that between the time you were twenty and a union leader in Mexico and the time you were chosen as a guest worker in the United States a few years ago that you were just plodding along as a common laborer? I don't believe it. You were probably serving time somewhere."

The two on the bed and the one on the floor jumped and shot Jennifer a double take. Alvarez came over to her and reached down with both hands to grab two of the chair legs. He stood quickly, pulling the chair from beneath her. Jennifer saw the room spin as she flew against the wall and slid to the floor, bruising her hip. "Where did you learn about me?" Alvarez shouted, and despite her fear and her aching hip, Jennifer smiled. It had just been a lucky guess.

When Alvarez boiled over at the sight of her smile and raised his fist, she held up a hand to wave him off. He turned to the others in the room and demanded to know who told her. No one responded. "I'll kill you, Benito!" he said. "Did you tell her? Luis? Maria?"

They all shook their heads and shook with fear. "They didn't tell me," Jennifer said. "It's just that there's a hole in your story, and prison is

Veiled Threat 59

written all over you. Tell me, was it in one of the horrible holes in Mexico or in the not-much-better U.S. federal pens in Texas or Oklahoma?"

He didn't answer.

"Texas, huh?" she tried. He glared, and she knew she was right. "Then you were an illegal alien at one time. Or tried to be. And you still are, am I right? Tell me what you really want of me and my readership."

"Money for my people," he said weakly, and she nearly laughed.

Jennifer stood and retrieved her own chair. "Pretty good trick," she said, feeling desperately, almost suicidally brave for some silly reason and knowing that she would be in for a good cry of relief if she ever got out of this. "Can you do it with someone your own size sitting in the chair?"

Alvarez looked as if he might try it again. Jennifer braced herself and decided to be ready to roll with the fall. But he backed away, eyeing her. She picked up her pen and pad. "I've decided I'm not going to write a column for you," she said. "You write it, put my name on it, deliver it, and see who in the United States publishes it."

Adolpho sat on the end of the bed and stared at Jennifer. "You are something else," he said, with no trace of a Spanish accent. "I spent almost ten years in a federal penitentiary in Louisiana for arranging for Mexicans to stay in the United States after their visitation visas had expired."

"Why weren't you deported?"

"I was born in New York."

Jennifer nodded. "And you met your wife where?"

"She is not my wife. She is my sister."

"And the Guest Workers Party?"

"You're looking at it."

"And your cause?"

"Hah!" Adolpho grunted derisively. "Our cause is money!"

"This is all motivated by greed?"

"Tell me who isn't greedy, lady! Let me tell you something. When our scheme to bring you here succeeded, when Benito and Luis came through that front door with you, our ship came in too. You are loved, you have money, the people who employ you have money, the people who read you have money. We need it. We want it. And we will have it!"

The other three faces showed fear and anticipation, wonder at the prospect of actually receiving money from the prize in the chair. "How much do you figure I'm worth?" Jennifer asked, genuinely curious.

Adolpho Alvarez was quick with his answer. "A quarter of a million dollars for each," he said.

"Only a million total?" Jennifer asked, pretending to be offended. "I'm in so many papers every day, you'd think you could get a few thousand from each one. Is that what we're going to do? You're going to write a

60   Jennifer Grey Mysteries

syndicated column-style ransom note to my family and friends and readers and employers, is that it?"

"You like it?" Adolpho asked. "I thought it was creative."

"I'll find out how much I'm worth, I guess. But tell me, how many papers do you think will cater to a terrorist?"

"What do you mean?"

"I mean, it's news that I'm missing, and the demands of my kidnappers is news. But would you devote a column to it if you were an editor or a publisher? I wouldn't. It would give too many crazies the same idea."

"You think I'm crazy?"

"Of course."

"You're going to wind up dead, you know that?"

"Because I tell the truth? The truth is what got me where I am today. Sitting here with four kidnappers. If I didn't tell the truth, you wouldn't have cared to kidnap me. I know one thing: I might be worth a million dollars to you alive. I'm worth nothing to you dead. Not one penny."

"That's why you have a smart mouth?"

"I guess. Don't think I'm not afraid of you or afraid for my family. But if you're going to do away with me anyway, I might as well get my last shots in, huh?"

"You would have done well as part of my team," Adolpho said.

"Don't count on it. I don't think you like people around you telling the truth too much. I do, however, have a suggestion of how best to handle this so-called writing assignment you've thrust on me."

"I'm listening."

"Let me do it straight. Let me tell the whole story, just as it's happened. Everything. The kidnapping, the lies, the fabricated cause, your story, the whole works. It'll all come down to the same thing. It may not be as noble a pursuit, but you can't deny that greed is your motivation. It'll be even more dramatic."

"What's in it for me?"

"It may work. Papers might run it. You might get your money—who knows?"

"What's in it for you?"

"I get to use all my creative energy telling the truth instead of making something up with a gun to my head. Or hands on my chair. And I get very few chances to tell my readers what makes me so foolishly brave sometimes. I can sure be forgiven for doing that here."

"What does make you so foolishly brave?" Adolpho asked.

"You'll have to read my column and find out."

"Will you use my real name?"

"I'd like to."

Veiled Threat

"I'd like you to. You see, we're going to succeed in this. And if it works out the way I hope, we will have no need to kill you. But one thing I want you to be very clear about. I have killed before. I. Me. I have killed with my bare hands. And I would do it again in a minute. If someone on the other end of this deal thinks I'm kidding or tries something cute, he'll find out. I'll deliver you to your public one piece at a time."

Jennifer's eyes showed that she had thought of another quick reply, but Maria quickly jumped in. "Mrs. Grey," she said, "I would humor A-A now. He is not kidding. He is serious. Your bravery has impressed him, but you will not humiliate him without paying a deep price."

"I want to be immortal," Adolpho said. "Don't you too, Benito and Luis? Maria?" They all nodded. "We will let her use our names, and we will take our money and escape, never to be found again. We will be the talk of the world until we die, and in our safe-deposit boxes in Argentina or Switzerland or wherever, we will reveal where we fled and how we lived on the greatest ransom payoff ever. No one will be able to duplicate it."

"Believe me," Jennifer said, "by tomorrow morning you will be one of the most famous men in America."

"And if that is true, and I have my money, you will be a free and happy and healthy woman. If there is a problem, you will die. You like truth. You live for truth. You write truth. You write that. That is truth."

Ten

The only calls that came through on Leo Stanton's phone at the *Day* during the next few hours were from George Knight, who had been informed by investigators at The Consulate that the command post had been shifted from the church to the newspaper office.

Finally, Jim was forced to promise him that he would keep him up-to-date at the first sign of any news. "Meanwhile, George," he said, "I have to tell you that no calls will be forwarded through to Mr. Stanton's phone unless they are from the kidnappers."

"Hoo, I hate that word," Mr. Knight said.

"Me too," Jim said.

"And I understand. Don't worry about us."

"I do worry about you," Jim said. "I worry about you and Jenn and Mrs. Knight."

"You can start calling us Mom and Dad pretty soon, you know."

"I should have been able to by now."

"You can if you'd like."

"I think I'd better wait."

"Suit yourself. But whatever you do, don't give up hope. We have the peace that passes all understanding."

"I'm glad to hear you say that. I'd appreciate it if you'd pray for me. I know Jennifer is uppermost in your mind, but this is very difficult for me."

"And for us, Jim. What say we pray for each other?"

Ellis was signaling Jim to free up the phone. And it wasn't long after he hung up that another call came through. Stanton put it on the speaker. The voice was muffled and statical, as if there was an intentionally bad connection and the caller was using a kerchief over the mouthpiece as well.

"There's gonna be a heavy delay, man, because we didn't have everything we needed for your columnist. We'll be callin' you back when we know where you can pick up the column."

"Listen!" Stanton said, "I couldn't understand you! Is that all you want? A column? Is that all?"

Veiled Threat 63

"You got it, man." And the line went dead. One of Ellis's technicians leaned through the door and shook his head. "Too quick," he said. "These guys are no dummies."

"How long do we have to still be able to make the morning paper?" Jim asked.

"A couple of hours," Stanton said, "but the problem is that we have to see the thing before we decide to print it."

"What do you mean?" Ellis asked. "If they demand you print something and you don't, Jennifer's life could be in danger."

"I know that, sir, and I happen to be a very close friend of hers besides being her boss so don't assume I don't have her best interests at heart. But there are considerations on any paper of this size and influence. We don't just publish anything and everything that someone tells us to, regardless of the situation. It might surprise you to know that I say yes or no on every column Jennifer writes, before it is sent to our syndicate and before it is printed in the *Day*."

"Have you ever said no?"

"Yes, sir, I have."

"On what grounds?"

"It's irrelevant here."

"I'll be the judge of that."

"Trust me, Sergeant Milton. I'm telling you that the reason I might have stopped a column or two in the past has no bearing on why we might or might not print the one we'll receive tonight."

"And I'm telling you that everything Mrs. Grey has written, published or not, could have an impact on this case. Irrelevant or not, you can tell me."

Stanton shook his head in resignation and pushed his half glasses up onto his forehead. He sat back in his chair and shifted his ever-present unlit cigar from one side of his mouth to the other. "Jennifer, as you may know, has some rather strongly held beliefs. When she is able to work them naturally into a column of broad appeal and interest, I let them go. When they become part and parcel of the column, the whole reason for it, I suggest more subtlety. Since she's become a sort of national media star, it has been harder and harder to talk her out of using her privileged platform position, if you will, as a soapbox for her religious beliefs."

"How does she respond?"

"Graciously. It would be inconsistent with her stand to blow up and get angry and throw things like some prima donnas I work with."

"But, I mean, what does she do about the column in question?"

"Usually, she rewrites it and works the pitch in naturally as an organic part of the whole."

64 Jennifer Grey Mysteries

"But she never leaves it out?"

"In those instances, no. Of course, only infrequently does this come into play."

"I understand. But it sounds to me like she's not the type to roll over and play dead just because someone suggests she try something different."

Both Jim and Leo laughed at the suggestion. Candy Atkins couldn't take it.

"I don't understand how you can laugh at a time like this! Who knows what is happening to Jennifer right now? Isn't there anything, something that can be done?"

"I wish there was, Candy," Ellis said. "Believe me, I wish there was. The problem is that we have so little to go on from what we've learned so far. We don't know where she is, which direction she went, who has her, or why. All we know is that she was taken and that a column is supposed to arrive soon."

"I feel so helpless," Candy said.

"We all do," Jim said.

"I'm afraid for Jennifer, but I'm afraid she's *not* afraid."

"I know what you mean, Candy. Jennifer has this sort of 'take-life-as-it-comes' mentality that lets her shoot back rather than be intimidated."

"Don't say 'shoot back,'" Candy said.

Ellis Milton was the only smoker in the bunch, Stanton being a cigar chewer rather than a puffer. The detective went through half a pack over the next few hours, filling the ashtray on Leo's desk. Candy paced and gulped coffee, making herself even more frazzled.

"I know it's a horrible thing to say at a time like this," she said, "but I think I'm getting hungry."

"Best suggestion I've heard all day," Ellis said. "I'm starving too. Would it offend anyone if we sent out for something?"

"I'll send someone," Leo said.

They were all munching sandwiches, all but Jim, when the phone rang. "Lincoln at Foster," came the heavy Spanish dialect. "You got it?"

Ellis Milton was frantically waving to Leo, telling him to stall.

"No, I don't have it!" Stanton said. "What did you say?"

"One more time, and that's it, man—take it or leave it. Lincoln at Foster!" Click.

Jim headed for the door. "Jim," Ellis said, "I've got to call downtown, and it's time to inform the FBI. You know kidnapping is a federal offense, even if they haven't crossed state lines. Now that they've named a drop-off point, we've got to inform that level."

Veiled Threat

65

"Let's just get going!" Jim said. "There's been no ransom figure discussed, nothing we have to do."

"Yes, there has! So far the ransom is the publishing of a column."

"But there's been no deal! We don't get Jennifer if we publish the column."

"No, but we're wide open to their threat on her health if we don't!"

"Well, call whoever you have to call, and let's get moving."

"Jim, you asked me to handle this, so you have to let me. You have to report to me, or I'll have someone downtown take you off the case. You shouldn't be in on it anyway. You're too close."

"El, don't do this to me."

"I will."

"Please."

"Then you are subordinate to me, regardless whether you agree with everything or not. You can have me taken off it too, I know, but they won't replace me with you. They'll replace me with someone who'd never dream of keeping you involved till it's over."

"Fair enough. I agree. Let's move."

"Just a minute."

Milton called police headquarters and requested that the FBI be informed. "Get some brass with clout to tell 'em we're just informing them at this point.... We don't want help or supervision or anything until we ask....I know, I know.... Just tell 'em that. Otherwise, I'll keep them in the dark too."

"I assume you want me to stay by the phone," Leo said.

"Exactly."

"I'm going," Candy said.

"Wrong," Ellis said.

"I can't just sit around here and—"

"Then go home! You're not going with us. I'm sorry. You've been a big help, and I don't mind your being in on things here, but this is a very dangerous mission. We don't know what we're getting into. We both have weapons, and we're prepared to use them. Do you and are you?"

She shook her head, almost in tears.

"Trust me, Candy. You'll help most by staying here."

Jim was the first through every door, first on the elevator, first off the elevator, first outside, first to the car, first in the car. Ellis hurried along behind him. He slid in behind the wheel. "Any bright ideas on the fastest way to get up there?"

"It's way up north, El. Probably the Kennedy to Lawrence and east."

"I think that's way out of the way, Jim. I think I'd get off at Western and go north. Sunday traffic won't be bad early in the evening."

66   Jennifer Grey Mysteries

"Whatever," Jim said, happy just to be moving.

It took Ellis a little less than twenty minutes to cruise up to Lincoln and Foster, and when he neared the corner, he told Jim he wasn't sure what he was looking for. "A manila envelope? A person? What?"

"Surely they wouldn't be stupid enough to send anyone. Then we'd be even. We'd have one of theirs; they'd have one of ours. Negotiations would be off."

"We won't be that lucky, but the turkey didn't tell us anything but the location. What does a newspaper column look like?"

"And who's this?" Jim said, nodding toward a black man walking along in the lengthening shadows from the hot sun.

"Just out for a stroll," Ellis said.

"I'm gonna watch him anyway," Jim said.

"Suit yourself."

Ellis was craning his neck to see if there was any obvious hiding or stashing place for an envelope or manuscript when the black man stepped into a phone booth and dug in his pocket. Before he could put a coin in, however, he picked up the phone and listened. He looked at the receiver and hung the phone up again. Then he placed his call, but said nothing and hung up.

Ellis was still looking behind them in the rearview mirror. Jim said, "El, pull over there by that guy." Milton popped a U-turn and rolled next to where the young black man would walk by. Jim rolled down his window but made no move as if to talk to the man.

As he walked by, he was shaking his head. Muttering to himself, he said, "Give me the girl's name, and I'll tell you where to look."

"What'd he say, Jim?" Ellis demanded.

Jim repeated it while reaching for the door handle. For once, Ellis was out of the car first, his gun in one hand, badge in the other. "Police!" he screamed. "Freeze!" Jim was out now and behind the man, both hands on his gun and in a low crouch, the weapon pointed at the man's face.

The black man froze all right. He almost fainted. "Hands in the air!" Milton shouted.

"Now over to the car and put 'em on the hood, feet back and spread 'em. C'mon, you've been through this before." Jim searched the man. "What is it, brothers?" he asked. "I ain't carryin' nothin'! I'm clean!"

"You got a name, sir?" Milton asked.

"Yes, sir. You wanna see my ID?"

"Later. Just tell me your name."

"Am I under arrest?"

"Do I have to put you under arrest to get your name? I will!"

"Luschel Bradley."

Veiled Threat

67

"What did you say when you walked by our car a second ago, Luschel?"

"I don't remember sayin' anything. I mighta been talkin' to myself."

"You tellin' me," Jim said, "that you don't remember saying, just a second ago, something about a girl's name and where to look?"

"Oh, that."

"Yeah! That!"

"The phone rang, man, just as I was gonna call my woman. I pick it up and a guy says that."

"Says what?"

"What I said. What'd I say? I don't remember."

"A guy says to tell him the girl's name and he'll tell you where to look?"

"Yeah."

"What'd he sound like?"

"Far away."

"Did he have an accent?"

"Yeah."

"Like?"

"Like maybe Puerto Rican."

"What'd you say to him?"

"I tol' him Gladys."

"Gladys!"

"Yeah, that's my woman. I figure maybe he's a Latin king or somethin' and he's got my woman. Scared me to death. 'Specially when I couldn't get her on the phone after that."

"What'd he say when you said 'Gladys?' "

"He said I was gonna regret that, and he hung up. I musta been runnin' that over in my mind when I walked by your car. Wrong thing to say, huh?"

"Sorry to detain you, Mr. Bradley. You're free to go."

"Man, this ain't my night," he said, wandering off. "Wonder where Gladys is."

The phone rang again. Milton ran and grabbed it. "What was that Gladys business?" came the telltale Mexican accent.

"That was an unfortunate coincidence. Now where's the column?"

"Give me the girl's name, and I'll tell you where to look."

"I mentioned the column and you still have to qualify me?"

"If you're tryin' to trace me, man, it ain't gonna work. I'm off of here now, but I'll call back in one minute. If the first thing I hear ain't the girl's name, she's dead." Milton slammed his fist on the metal counter.

"What?" Jim wanted to know.

"I almost blew it, that's all," Ellis said. "He'll call back, and I'll play it his way. I just hate to cater to punks. I've been through all the training,

68   Jennifer Grey Mysteries

know what to say and what not to say. But treating them with kid gloves while they're threatening someone, scaring 'em to death, and playing mind games with us, that goes against my grain."

"Play it straight, please."

"I will, I will." The phone rang. "Jennifer!" Ellis said quickly.

"Greyhound Bus Station—downtown," the voice said.

"Where in the station, man? That's a big place!"

Click.

Eleven

The column had taken Jennifer more than two hours to write, and amazingly—she thought—Adolpho Alvarez had asked her to change only details that would have led the police to his door. He made her change the color and general description of the vehicle she was transferred to after her car was dumped in Lake Michigan, and he had her change the reference from Lake Michigan to the Chicago River.

Other than that, she had written the story exactly as it happened, from the bogus phone call to just missing running over Benito Diaz. She described the weapon he carried, the meeting with Luis, and the pushing of the car into the "river." She added a line at the end of that episode that slipped past her abductors, but which she hoped and prayed would not slip past her loved ones, her editor, her readers, and the police.

It was just one of those creative throwaway lines she used frequently to add spice to her writing. "My heart sank with my beautiful new car that Jim and I had already enjoyed so much. My only hope was that the alewives would appreciate it as much as we had."

Astute readers would catch the clue. Alewives were a Lake Michigan problem. They covered the beaches during the bad years for such fish. But Jennifer prayed that not only would Leo and Jim and whoever else was involved pick up on the obvious error, but that they would also comb the column for other clues. She realized that her only hope was to use her God-given ability to put words together. God had provided her best chance at escaping, and it lay within that brand spanking new typewriter Adolpho Alvarez was so proud of.

In describing her abductors, she wrote that Luis was "to me a cross between an Apache, a Sioux, and maybe a Cuban. He is a tall, lanky, hauntingly handsome man of slow pace and a certain dark grace. A follower. A doer. A thinker rather than a talker. Obedient. He'll do anything A-A tells him to do."

She described her ordeal thus far:

I could as easily be writing an epic I'd call "My Experiences in the World War," and here I am only hours into my dilemma. I keep asking myself, *How did it happen? Why did it happen?*

70 Jennifer Grey Mysteries

What did I miss? Could I or should I have known that the first telephone call from the hotel was a bogus one?

There's something about the experience that is as embarrassing as it is frightening. It's that sort of hate yourself feeling that comes with a public goof like a run in your pantyhose or having your picture taken with the hole showing in the bottom of your shoe. I've heard people say that when they've been robbed they feel as if they've been violated or their privacy has been invaded. I know the feeling now. And the questions. I keep asking myself the questions . . .

She told the whole story of the charade and how she was able to cut through the baloney and get Adolpho to admit that his was not a cause of justice or a torch for humankind, the working man, or anyone else except himself and his small band of members of the "Guest Workers Party of the United Mexican States."

In fact, I sit a bit stunned, amazed actually, yet knowing that the man has an ego that will let me write that he *has* such an ego without fear of reprisal. It isn't that he isn't a violent man or that he won't make good on his death threat if his demands are not met; it's just that he has a thirst for power and glory and immortality—worth gaining even through infamy—that is nearly as unquenchable as his greed. He reminds me a bit of Clyde Barrow of "Bonnie and Clyde" fame, who was so deeply touched by his girlfriend's poems that chronicled their reign of terror. Even the lines memorializing those who were foolish enough to try to stop them and wound up dead in the process were precious to Clyde, because he had been immortalized on the front pages of papers all over the United States and Europe.

I am not without fear, that gut-wrenching, almost immobilizing terror that reminds you that you could be here today and gone tomorrow, and were it not for my deep belief that God is in control and that my future is secure with Him, I know I would be unable to function at all, even to maintain my composure, let alone to write.

For it is this God alone who is worthy of praise and power, and it is He alone who holds the keys to true immortality. Not the immortality that lets a Clyde Barrow live on in poetry and legend decades after his death, or a Julius Caesar for centuries after his,

Veiled Threat

but rather the real thing, the actual, bona fide, eternal living immortality that allows a person to never really die.

Jennifer even wrote of her sarcasm and dark humor.

I dreaded and hated myself for it even as it was coming out of my mouth. But that too, I sensed, was born of a belief that I was where I was supposed to be and doing what I was supposed to be doing. When a man twice my size in anger literally pulls my chair from under me and I see not only the ceiling and the walls whiz by but also my brief life and the face of my soon-to-be husband, yet still I am able to call my captor a coward and write the same for many hundreds of thousands of reading eyes, then I know that either I am the most foolish woman ever to breathe or I have been gifted with a power outside myself.

Don't think that if you read of my death tomorrow, or the next day, that my faith has been in vain. Neither blame God for all my boldness, for no doubt much of it has been ill-timed and not so carefully conceived (an understatement, I realize, as I put it on paper).

While it is of some comfort to me to be in the familiar mode of writing to you as I do several times a week, I am using equipment that is unfamiliar to me. I am writing from a posture of pressure and fear that I wouldn't wish on anyone. And lest anyone think there is anything glamorous or positive about this experience, please know that no matter how it seems, you would not want to trade places with me, regardless of what may come of it.

I admit I have envied reporters who have voluntarily inserted themselves into dangerous situations to help work out solutions. I have also questioned their motives and assumed them glory-seekers. But now that I have experienced that deep, mortal fear that battles constantly against my faith, I know they could have had such surface motives only the first time, never again.

For when a weapon is pressed against your cheek and you can feel the cold steel and smell the acrid oil and imagine the sound and the result of the explosion in the chamber that you would never hear, you know that this is not cops and robbers in the backyard. This is not a TV show or a movie. This is it. This is life and death in the cold, stark reality of ugly weapons, selfish motives, and nothing-left-to-lose characters who risk their precious anonymity, their freedom, their futures for one big

72 Jennifer Grey Mysteries

payoff, one booty of a million dollars in small, unmarked bills to be split four ways.

The question, of course, is one which must be faced by the principals. Can they trust each other? Will a man who would mastermind a kidnapping, concoct a story about fighting for the working man, use the platform of a newspaper columnist, and terrorize her friends and family and co-workers in the process, not make some attempt to skip out with their share of the money?

Adolpho had enjoyed that paragraph. In his perverse way, he had taken delight in the possibilities that he was worse than he appeared, that there was no honor among thieves, at least not when this thief was tossed into the mix. But it was the next paragraph that caused him some grief and which changed his strategy. He would send two pickup people rather than one.

Should Double-A, the noble wolf, be noble enough to trust whoever he sends out to pick up the ransom? Or will he be able to send only his own flesh and blood? And can he trust her? That, of course, is when he will be most vulnerable. Will the pickup person return?

When he or she returns, will the split be equal? Will A-A then uphold his end of the bargain and deal with the payers?

Were it not I here in this situation, but rather some nameless, faceless columnist from some other daily newspaper, I might assert that the missionary agencies in South America have the best policy. They do not pay. They do not cater. They do not bend or bow. They lose missionaries too, but they believe—and probably rightly so—that they will lose those missionaries anyway. They do not trust the abductors. They could pay and still see their people killed. In fact, that is more likely.

That could happen here too. I hope it does not. Not because I don't believe that my afterlife is secure with God, but because I cannot bear to think of the grief it would cause my family and my fiancé. I enjoy my life, my love, my people, the place I work. I don't fear death, but I fear dying. I want to stay around until I'm 90 and then slip peacefully away in my sleep.

So, yes, it's selfish, this personal change of policy. I don't want my friends and family and newspaper maintaining lofty ideals and refusing to be moved to spend the money necessary to win my release. I promise to help in every way to find my abductors, but get me out of here first.

Veiled Threat

As I've said, I can't guarantee that they'll deal fairly, but since it's me, since it's someone I've grown close to over the years, since I have a personal, vested interest in the abducted, I'd rather not see a reaction that flies in the face of the captors and gives them no choice but to prove their mettle. There is something to be said for following the best police psychology of the day when dealing with short-fused, volatile people.

These words, I assure you to the best of my ability, I wrote on my own, without coercion. Only a few facts, protecting the location of my captivity, were adjusted. The following I write under instructions from the noble wolf, whom I would not describe that way, were I given the choice. (You see? He still allows me latitude even here.)

The payoff figure is 1 million dollars in small, unmarked bills. Forty-eight hours are allowed to raise it. A drop-off point will be phoned to the offices of the *Chicago Day* before dark on Tuesday night. If the pickup person either does not return to Adolpho Alvarez or there is any evidence that he or she has been followed, I will be killed. No question. No hesitation.

I'm back, on my own. I know my column is much longer than normal, that it will not fit on the front page of the *Day* and that many of my regular papers will not carry it because they choose not to. It's not only because they thought I was to be off for the next three weeks, but rather because they do not cater to a criminal element.

But to those who carry it, I'm grateful. I had hoped that at least this would be a daily dialogue between my captors and the ransom payees, but perhaps this is best. Two days seems long enough to put off the inevitable. Something will happen; I hope no one is hurt. Most of all, I admit, I hope I am not hurt.

Should it turn out for the worst for me, either due to my paper or my family or the police being unwilling or unable to accede to the demands of the kidnappers, please know that I understand. Forgive the personal addresses in my column which, as a rule as you know, I avoid wherever possible.

But Jim, I love you. Mom and Dad, I love you. Leo, I love you. My church friends, I love you. Most of all I love my Savior, Christ, and I know that to be with Him is far better. I believe that, though I won't really *know* it until I get there. Forgive the morbidity of these final few thoughts, and accept my greetings

74   Jennifer Grey Mysteries

and expressions as sincerely and with as many heart feelings as they are offered.

Benito Diaz returned from the bus station downtown with the news of the misfire on the first phone call. "I couldn't believe it," he said. "Some dude tellin' me Jennifer's name was Gladys. I thought they were tryin' to do a number on me."

For only the second time since the beginning, Jennifer thought she saw some nervousness, some weakening in Adolpho. He paced more. He sat with his head in his hands. He seemed distracted. He looked at his watch. He kept asking Maria what was next.

"I don't know," she would tell him. "They get it at the bus station, they read it, they decide if they're gonna print it, they decide if they're gonna get the money and wait for our call."

"And we call 'em when the sun goes down Tuesday night," Alvarez said, "right? Is that right?"

She nodded.

"And should we have another column ready for Tuesday morning's paper? Something Jennifer would write tomorrow night?"

Luis and Benito looked at each other and then at Maria. It was clear to Jennifer that none of them was as comfortable with being immortalized in the papers as Adolpho was. They didn't look enthusiastic.

"How about you?" A-A asked Jennifer.

She shrugged. "I do what I'm told," she said.

"But do you want to?"

"I don't know what else I'd write. Unless I brought everybody up-to-date on my daily activities. What are we going to do tomorrow?"

She meant it as a joke, but Adolpho was tired and irritable. He didn't appreciate her sarcasm anymore. It didn't impress him the way it had earlier. "Sometimes," he said icily, "I hope they don't honor our demands and that it ends up in a big shoot-out and you go down with us in a blaze of gunfire."

Jennifer didn't respond. She could tell he meant it. He continued.

"And you *would* go down with us, because you would be the first person I would shoot. I would take Benito's Uzi, and I would turn you into hamburger and sling you out the door. And if the odds were against me, I would kill myself before I would let anyone else kill me."

"Your own people might kill you first," Jennifer said softly. Double-A heard her but pretended he didn't.

"Get some sleep," he advised. "There will be someone outside your door all night."

Jennifer went to bed exhausted, but too keyed up to sleep. She was miserable. She heard muffled conversations from the living room where Adolpho was working and reworking strategy, trying to determine if he or his sister should accompany one of the others for the all-important pickup.

Jennifer fought the stinging tears that welled up in her eyes. She knew she had to be strong, that wasting tears now would be useless unless the clues she planted in her column were successful. Would they bring rescuers to her, or would she have to take her chances with police strategy centered around the money drop?

All she could do was pray, and all she could think to pray was that by morning someone would also be outside Adolpho's door.

Twelve

Ellis Milton and Jim Purcell parked illegally downtown and raced into the Greyhound Bus Terminal, not knowing what or whom to look for. But they looked anyway. They ran up and down the corridors, in and out the doors, past the game rooms, past the cafeteria, past the waiting rooms and the benches and the vending machines.

They ran past the ticket counters, looking everywhere—up, down, sideways, in people's faces. All they got were blank stares, some half smiles. Jim and Ellis slowed and almost stopped several times when they saw someone who looked like Jennifer or who fit the description of the young Latino she had almost run down in the street in front of the church.

They looked in phone booths, and even in a few buses. "We're getting nowhere," Jim huffed and puffed at last.

"I know," the sweating and panting detective said. "We have to stop and think. Where *should* we look for something?"

They stood staring at each other, then at the ceilings and walls and people.

"Lost and found," Ellis said. "Make any sense?"

"Not much," Jim said. "But I'll try anything."

At the lost and found center, Ellis asked if there was anything there for a Jim Purcell.

"Like what?" the man asked.

"A manuscript, an envelope, a folder. Something like that?"

"Nope. Only envelope I got here is for a—ah—just a second—yeah, Grey—J. Grey."

"That's it!" Jim and Ellis shouted in unison.

"That's what?" the man asked. "You didn't say anything about a J. Grey."

"We've got no time to argue, pal," Ellis said, whipping out his badge as Jim did the same. "Just give me the envelope and tell me where to sign, and I'll take full responsibility."

"I'll have to see a driver's license."

"You'll see nothin' but a badge number. Now let's have it!"

In the car, Jim discarded the envelope and dusted the inside pages for fingerprints. They had all been wiped clean. "Crafty," he said. By the time he and Ellis got back to the *Day* Jim had read the column aloud three times by the dim light inside the car. Every time he finished it, he slammed his palms on the dashboard.

"I don't see *anything* in here!" he said. "I mean it's an incredible story, but wouldn't she be trying to tip us off? Does our picking it up at the bus station mean they've taken her somewhere at least a bus ride away? What do you get from it?"

"Nothing yet. But you know her better than I do. Would she try to give you clues?"

"Of course! The only thing that doesn't make sense is that line about the fish in the Chicago River. I mean, there may be alewives there, but you never think of that. You associate them with Lake Michigan."

"Then she is giving you a clue!"

"Maybe, but what does it mean? So what if she was trying to say it was Lake Michigan and not the Chicago River. It doesn't help us."

"Maybe she's just telling you that every detail in the story is slightly inaccurate."

"But that doesn't help either."

"It helps her, Jim. Later she can show how she disassociated herself from the phony story."

"But that will be meaningless unless we can free her! Otherwise there won't be a 'later.'"

"Take it easy, guy. If there are clues there, we have people who can find them. Does she try to tell you anything by using the first letter of each sentence to form a word, anything like that?"

Jim studied the piece again. "Nah. Anyway, her abductors would have checked for that, wouldn't they?"

"I don't know. She doesn't exactly paint a picture of them as being too bright, does she?"

"Oh, no," Ellis said as he pulled into the *Day* lot and saw a dozen marked and unmarked squad cars from various agencies. "We've got all the help we need now."

"What's this all about?" Jim asked.

"Who knows? Somebody tipped 'em, and now they all want in on the act."

From the lobby Ellis phoned Leo. "I'm sorry," the editor said. "Once it got out over the wire and the radio and TV news guys got a hold of it, we were dead. It's been on the air for more than an hour, the whole thing, promising news of her column to come, all that. Did you get it?"

Jennifer Grey Mysteries

"Yeah, we got it, and we're gonna need help deciphering it. Can you start a copy machine smokin'?"

"Not until I've read it."

"I'm not asking you to decide on putting it in the paper. Whether you do that or not, we need to see if she gave us any clues. Though if you decide against printing it, you'll have to have a pretty good reason."

Phones were ringing all over the place when they got to Stanton's office. He was taking no calls from reporters on other newspapers. "As for the other law enforcement agencies," he said, "Sergeant Milton, they're all yours."

And Ellis took over. He announced that the case was his from the beginning and that unless he heard from his own immediate superior or above, he was still in charge, and any and all activity had to be assigned by him or cleared through him.

"Do you have the column?" someone asked.

"Yes."

"What are you going to do with it?"

"The *Day* editor is perusing it now. Then he'll copy it for anyone who wants to help us determine if she has planted any clues for us."

"*If?* What do you mean *if?* If she didn't, she's got to be nuts."

"Or maybe she's being careful," Ellis said.

"There's such a thing as being too careful."

"Not with the group that has her, gentlemen."

"Well, we wouldn't know, would we?"

"Patience."

Jim and Ellis checked in on Leo, who was handing pages to Candy as he finished them. "This is great stuff," she said. "I mean, just the writing itself."

"It's her all right," Leo said.

"It is?" Ellis asked.

"You're sure?"

"No doubt about it."

"No irregularities?"

"Plenty."

"You make anything of them?"

"Plenty."

"Really?"

Leo didn't answer. He quieted Milton with a wave of his hand as he finished the last few pages. "Let me speed read 'em again when you're through, Candy," he said. "Just to be sure."

"Can we copy them first and get others working on them?"

Veiled Threat

"In a minute," Leo said.

"We don't have a minute, sir. Can it be run in the paper?"

"Yes, in ours."

"In others?"

"It's up to each one. I'm guessing they'll run it with the full story of the disappearance. Most will only say that I believe the column is from her. We can't guarantee it."

"But you're sure?"

"I'd stake my life on it."

"Read fast, and tell me what you think," Milton said.

Candy confided that she had seen nothing in the column that gave her any hint where Jennifer might be. Leo handed the pages to Ellis. "Have Marge, outside, make as many copies as you want. But none—repeat, *none*—may leave this building."

"So, what did you find?"

Leo smiled faintly. "I'd rather withhold my guess until the others have a chance to corroborate it without any knowledge of what I'm thinking."

"All due respect, sir, but we don't have time for games."

"I'm not trying to play a game, Sergeant. I really need to know that I haven't planted ideas in people's minds that may not have been there otherwise."

When Ellis started handing out the copies to the various representatives of the local, state, and federal agencies, one commander said, "I need four copies. I brought along two cryptologists and a trivia buff."

"That's three."

"Include me too."

"What are your qualifications?"

"I read Jennifer Grey religiously."

It didn't take the cryptologists long to determine that no traditional or recently devised letter or word patterns had been used to transmit a message. One of them immediately noticed the mention of the alewives in the Chicago River, but when he mentioned it aloud, several others scolded him.

"We've all got that," they said. "But there has to be more."

Many of the cops and their aides were studying every word, looking each up in the dictionary and asking Stanton for access to reference books and maps. During the second hour of study, Stanton had the entire column transmitted over the news wires to hundreds of papers across the country who typeset it for morning editions. The *Day* itself would hit the streets at 4:30 A.M.

80 Jennifer Grey Mysteries

Finally, both a state police criminologist and a federal agent sat back and tossed their pencils down. "Giving up?" Ellis asked.

"Nope," one said, smiling. "We think we know where she is."

"So do we," came the response from a small cluster in another corner.

Candy and Leo emerged from his office. Jim stood. "Who wants to be first?"

"We think she's trying to tell us that the car is in Lake Michigan and she is at the Stevenson Expressway and Pershing."

"That's what I thought!" Leo said.

"Us too!" another group piped in.

"Where did you get that?" Jim said, shaking his head. But Ellis was dragging him to the door.

"Listen up, everyone!" the detective said. "If it's that clear to all of you, I have to buy it, even if I don't know how you did it. I also have to think there'll be a lot of amateur detectives reading the column who might beat us over there if we don't hurry."

By the time everyone was assigned locations at the stakeout and a vehicle with sophisticated communications capabilities was appropriated from downtown, it was near dawn. The *Day* had hit the streets, and a couple of national radio news networks had read the column on the air.

Ellis was right. As law enforcement officers began slowly converging on the only building at Pershing and the Stevenson, crowds had begun to gather. "There goes our hope of catching three of them asleep," Ellis moaned.

"I don't believe this," Jim said, pointing out a group of Mexicans who carried handpainted signs reading "Mexicans Against Alvarez" and "Free Jennifer Grey."

"Where did they get the time to do that?" he asked. "Now all we need is for them to start chanting and blowing our cover."

Uniformed policemen cordoned off the area and kept the crowds back while Ellis and Jim planned surreptitious entry to the building. "It looks impregnable from here," Jim said.

"Worse," Ellis said. "We don't know who, if anyone, is in there."

"Don't bail out on all that expert help now," Jim said. "They couldn't have all come to the same conclusion by coincidence."

Just the same, Ellis assigned someone to see if a phone had been installed in the building. One had. The number was unlisted. Which meant it took the police a few minutes longer to get it. The billing went to AA, Inc., and the majority of the long distance calls in the last month had been placed to New York.

Veiled Threat

81

Ellis and three other plainclothes detectives from the Chicago PD approached the building from the angle of each of its corners. There were no windows. Just the garage door, securely locked, and a service door that had apparently been sealed shut.

"A clear violation of the fire code," Ellis radioed back to Jim in a command car.

Jim shrugged and looked at Ellis's watch commander, Lieutenant Steve Sykes, who had just arrived. Sykes deadpanned, "So what's he gonna do— bust 'em on a code violation or set the place on fire?"

When the four had all scrambled back to the safety of the car, Ellis reported: "I don't think we were seen or heard, but there's no way of getting in there by force without waking the dead. And I don't think they're gonna fall for any phony stuff in person."

"Then what?" Jim asked.

"Maybe they'll fall for something by phone."

"Like what?"

"Like this." Ellis dialed the unlisted number from the phone in the car. "You know Alvarez is not going to answer, so I've got a one in two chance of guessing right if a man answers. If it's a woman, it has to be Maria, right?"

Everyone nodded and held their breath. The phone rang three times, then a groggy voice whispered, "Hello?"

"Hey, Benito!" Ellis said urgently in a beautifully faked accent. "It's Chico from New York, man. I gotta talk to Double-A fast."

"This ain't Benito, Chico. This is Luis. Do I know you?"

"I don't think so, Luis, but I heard a lot about you from Adolpho. I know it's early, man, but can you get 'im?"

"Jes' a minute."

Ellis held up his free hand and crossed his fingers. Several minutes passed. Then came the voice of Adolpho Alvarez. "This is the noble wolf," he said, sounding still asleep. "Who is this?"

"This is Chicago Police Department Detective Sergeant Ellis Milton, Adolpho. I want you to listen carefully and be prepared to deal. Are you awake, sir?"

There was no response, but neither did Adolpho hang up. "I am going to assume you can hear me, sir," Ellis continued. "You are surrounded, with no possibility of escape. You have little time and no options. Can you hear me?"

The only sound from the other end was rapidly accelerating breathing. "Sir?" Ellis called. "Señor Alvarez?"

82   Jennifer Grey Mysteries

Suddenly, Adolpho was screaming, but not into the phone. "I don't believe this!" he shouted to his people. "Get her up! Get her out of bed! They're going to make me kill her! Get her up! Get her up!"

"Adolpho!" Ellis shouted. "Adolpho! Listen to me! There's no need to do anything rash. Let's talk! Let's deal!"

Finally, Adolpho acknowledged Milton. "No talkin'!" he yelled into the phone. "You said we can't escape and we got no options, man. Remember, *you're* the one who said it! We're gonna show you what kind of options we've got! You ever heard of an Uzi?"

"Yes, sir, but there's no reason to—"

"Shut up!" and he slammed down the phone. The command officers began organizing everyone into a huge circle around the building. They were back more than fifty feet and hiding behind cars. The crowd was pushed farther and farther back until everyone was outside the range of gunfire.

"Get some lights flashing!" Ellis hollered. "When he looks out to see if we're serious, I want it to look like Christmas."

Lights began flashing all around the building, and spotlights were trained on the garage door. "It's got to come up!" Ellis said. "It's the only way he can see us."

He was right. It came up about halfway, automatically, and was lowered quickly. When there was no activity from inside for almost four minutes, Ellis called the number again. Before he could say anything, Adolpho picked up the phone.

"I'm comin' out with the girl!" he said, "and my people will be behind me. I'm gonna have the weapon at her throat, and here's what I want. I want a helicopter and one unarmed pilot to take us to O'Hare and an empty jet with one unarmed pilot waiting for us. You got that?"

Ellis didn't respond. His watch commander pantomimed that he should at least pretend to accede to every request, and they would deal with it later.

"OK, all right," Ellis said. "It'll take a while. Just be cool."

"It'd better be fast. Anything goes wrong—*anything*—she's a dead woman." And he hung up.

Ellis turned to Commander Sykes. "I'm sorry, sir, but I don't think that is the way to handle this guy. I know all the stuff about what to say and what not to say, but why cater to him? We can't deliver the 'copter and the jet, so why lead him on and pretend we can? Just to keep him from getting riled? He's riled already! How do you think he'll react when he finds out we've been lying to him?"

Veiled Threat   83

The commander pursed his lips."You know department policy, Ellis, and—"

"I know we're gonna wind up with someone dead in there if you don't let me talk his language, Lieutenant."

"Meaning?"

"Trust me."

"It's all on your shoulders, Ellis, but I won't back you up."

"But you'll let me handle it?"

"I'll deny it later."

"But you won't stop me now?"

"You're on your own."

"That's all I wanted to hear," Ellis said as he dialed Adolpho again.

Thirteen

Adolpho answered, "*What!* If the chopper ain't comin', I don't wanna hear from you!"

"The chopper ain't comin', Adolpho, but you'd better listen to me."

"Talk!"

"You wanna deal?"

"You know what I want, man!"

"Yes, I do, Adolpho, and you're not going to get it. The deal will be my deal. It will be the only deal offered, and you can take it or leave it."

"Listen, man! I'm gonna—"

"No, you listen, and listen carefully, 'cause I'm only runnin' this down once. I call the shots here. I set the deals—not you. Now *we've* got lots of time. But you're limited by how much food you've got. We're gonna wait until you come out. I want you to surrender, to send Mrs. Grey out first, unharmed. Then I want you and your people to come out one at a time— six feet apart—you first, hands on your head. Leave your weapons inside. You got it?"

"Have I got it? That's *it?* That's no deal!"

"That's the only deal you're gonna get."

"What's in it for me, man?"

"This is what's in it for you, Adolpho. This is the deal, total and on the table, OK? If Mrs. Grey comes out unharmed, you come out unharmed and charged only with those crimes you have committed thus far. If you hurt her, we will hurt you. If you kill her, we will kill you. That's it. You decide."

And Ellis Milton turned off the phone, trembling. Commander Sykes sat in the backseat, palms cupping his temples, shaking his head.

The next twenty minutes crept by as the sun rose higher in the sky, and Jim Purcell sat in a pool of his own sweat, praying and hoping that Ellis had done the right thing.

The strategy went against everything they all knew about the psychology of dealing with an irrational, demented, violent terrorist. Jim shivered, imagining he heard a burst of automatic weapon fire inside the building. Had he imagined it? Was it real? If it was real, was it his beloved

Veiled Threat

85

being made an instant martyr to a bad cause? Had Adolpho turned the weapon on himself! Or had one of his people murdered him?

Jim looked at his colleagues and sympathetic friends. And he realized that he had only imagined the sound. And then he imagined it again and again—until it was killing *him*, and he wished the bullets, real or imagined, were ripping through him, ending his nightmare. He didn't know how much longer he could bear the agony.

"Should you call him again, El?" he asked weakly. "What if he has a question, needs clarification? He doesn't know how to call you."

Ellis was pale. "He doesn't *need* to call me, Jim. I couldn't have been clearer. He's thinking. That's all I could have hoped for. The deal's the same now as it was twenty minutes ago, and it'll be the same twenty-four hours from now."

"I could never last," Jim whined. "What if he's killed everyone and himself?"

"That's what would have happened if we had stormed the place."

"Ellis, I can't help but think this is a reckless, dangerous move."

"No move I could have made would have been less dangerous, Jim. He has a no-win situation. I couldn't pretend to open a window of hope to him. I talked his language; he understood me. The rest is in his hands."

"That's what bothers me. The man least capable of making the right decision will determine what happens here."

"It was going to be that way no matter what. The terrorist always holds the trump card. But I set the parameters, Jim. The decision is his, but he's deciding between the options I gave him."

Jim felt as if he had to get out of the car, but he didn't know where he'd go. He wanted to pray, but he didn't know what he'd say. He wanted to take charge, but he didn't know what he'd do. He wanted to punch Ellis, but he knew in his heart of hearts that, right or wrong, Ellis had the same goal in mind that he had.

But it was *his* fiancée in there! It was his life, his love, his future. The helplessness and hopelessness of it all ate away at his bones and his brain.

At first, Jim had hoped and prayed and longed to see that door open and Jennifer come running out to him. But with every additional second, that hope seemed more and more remote until it was a foolish kid's dream, mocking him, making him feel the fool, the dunce, the joker. To think it would all turn out the way he wanted it, the way Ellis had laid it out!

Such trash! It would end in bloodshed. Jim prayed, *God forgive these thoughts! It's hopeless. I can't stand it! How long will he wait? How long can I wait?*

86 **Jennifer Grey Mysteries**

"Ellis!" Jim said too loudly, making everyone jump. "What if he hurts or kills Jennifer and he comes out first, and you don't know what's happened to her until he's in custody?"

Ellis didn't respond.

"You can't take justice into your own hands then, can you, El?"

"I might have to, to keep my word."

"It would be the end of your badge," Sykes said.

"I wouldn't be able to live with myself if I let him get away with something like that anyway," Ellis said. "What's the difference how I end my career?"

"But, Ellis," Jim said, "I'm serious. What will you do?"

"If he comes out first, I'll drop him on the spot."

"But don't you owe it to him to warn him of that?"

"Jim! I owe him nothing! I told him the rules. If he breaks the rules, he'll suffer for it. If he comes out first, I can only assume that Jennifer is hurt."

"But maybe—"

"But nothing! Maybe nothing! She *must* come out first and reach us unharmed for him to be alive by the end of the day."

Weapons were trained on the garage door. Jim had to get out of the car. He pulled his gun from its holster and crouched behind the left rear fender. Ellis joined him with a bullhorn.

Without warning, the garage door opened, and hammers were pulled back on a hundred pistols. Ellis managed all the coolness and calmness he could in spite of the raspy loudness of the speaker as he said, "Easy, easy, easy—hold your fire, hold it, hold it, hold it."

And Jennifer emerged alone. She was dressed in her own clothes, and her hands were empty, her arms limp at her sides. She walked steadily toward a police car at right angles to where Jim and Ellis crouched. Jim wanted to shout, to run to her, to embrace her, to cry, to pray. He started to move, but Ellis's vice grip caught his arm. "We're not out of the woods yet."

Jennifer looked as if she wanted to run, to dive for cover, but she fought the urge. She could have been walking down the aisle, the way she forced herself to step slowly, carefully, methodically.

"Easy, Jennifer," Ellis intoned. "That's it."

When she reached the exposed side of the squad car, two uniformed policemen scampered out and pulled her between cars and to the ground where she burst into tears. They helped her crawl into the back seat and lie down. Shortly, the squad car pulled away.

When Jim turned back to the scene, the muscular Adolpho Alvarez was slowly walking across the same path, his hands on top of his head, no

Veiled Threat

87

weapon visible. Not far behind came the lanky Luis Cardenas in the same posture, his face showing no emotion. Six feet in back of him was the petite Maria Ruiz, her eyes puffy and red, hands on her head, feet moving in double time to match the speed of the men.

It was her speed that made it less noticeable when Benito Diaz did not emerge at the proper interval. Ellis had been coaxing them along slowly with the bullhorn, soothing them, encouraging them, keeping his men calm at the same time.

Two officers stood to come around and meet Adolpho, but they froze when Ellis shouted through the bullhorn, "Wait for the other! Wait till he shows himself!"

And from inside the dark garage rang out the burp of six shots that tore through Adolpho Alvarez's spinal cord and heart and left him time only to wrench his hands from his head in an effort to break his fall.

But midway through his descent, the power source connecting his brain to his muscles had been severed, and he crashed face first onto the pavement. He appeared as if he would have twisted to get a look at his slayer, if he'd had the choice.

Policemen dived for cover, and Luis and Maria ran in opposite directions, their hands still in the air, pleading for the men not to shoot. Ellis was still on the bullhorn. "Wait, wait, wait—don't shoot, don't return fire, hold your fire."

The Uzi came clattering out of the garage into the dirt, Benito proudly following it, standing upright, head held high, empty hands atop his head. He walked straight to where Adolpho lay and screamed, "Coward!" at the corpse as he was taken into custody.

Jim slumped to the ground, his back to the bumper of the unmarked squad that contained Lieutenant Steve Sykes, the ashen-faced watch commander of Ellis Milton. And Jim wept.

EPILOGUE

The sleepy-eyed Jennifer was glad to see Jim at police headquarters. They held each other, long and silently, burying their faces in each other's necks. Later, when they were alone, they would praise God for His miraculous protection. Jennifer was eager to reset the wedding date for the next Sunday—after they'd both had some rest, and she was shocked to hear of Alvarez's death.

Still she was able to smile when Jim asked, "Is anyone going to tell me how Jennifer led us to her?"

"I would have thought you would be the first to catch it," she said. "John J. Pershing's memoirs were entitled *My Experiences in the World War*, and if there was any doubt, I said Luis looked like an Apache, a Sioux, and a Cuban. Which is ridiculous. No one could look like both an American Indian and a Cuban. But Pershing's first three tours of duty were in the Apache campaign, the Sioux campaign, and in Cuba."

"So that put you on Pershing Street," Jim said. "A big, long street."

"And the most famous picture of a hole in the sole of a shoe was taken of the foot of Adlai Stevenson."

"Thus," Jim said, "the Stevenson Expressway at Pershing."

"Right."

"Pretty obscure."

"Apparently, not to everyone—fortunately for me."

"And me," Jim said.

Dear Reader:

Please let us know how you feel about Barbour Books' Christian Fiction.

1. What most influenced you to purchase Jennifer Grey Mystery Collection #1, #2, #3 (Please circle one)?

   _____ Author   _____ Recommendations

   _____ Subject matter   _____ Price

   _____ Cover / titles

2. Would you buy other books in the Jennifer Grey Mystery series by this author?

   _____ Yes   _____ No

3. Where did you purchase this book?

   _____ Christian book store   _____ Other

   _____ General book store   _____ Mail order

4. What is your overall rating of this Collection?

   _____ Excellent _____ Very good _____ Good _____ Fair _____ Poor

5. How many hours a week do you spend reading books? _____ hrs.

6. Are you a member of a church? _____ Yes _____ No

   If yes, what denomination?_____

7. Please check age

   _____ Under 18   _____ 25-34   _____ 45-54

   _____ 18-24   _____ 35-44   _____ 55 and over

> Mail to: **Fiction Editor**
> **Barbour Books**
> P.O. Box 1219
> Westwood, NJ 07675

NAME ————————————————————————

ADDRESS ——————————————————————

CITY ——————————— STATE ———— ZIP ————

Thank you for helping us provide the best in Christian fiction!